CW01635892

Twin Trouble

Jayne Osborne

Published in 2014 by FeedARead.com Publishing

A CIP catalogue record for this title is available from the British Library.

Dedicated to the members of the Cross Stitch Guild

With grateful thanks for the friendship over the years.

Chapter One

"That man is doing my head in" Katrina said as she entered the office, and sat down at the desk. "What's he done now?" her deputy asked with a smile, but Katrina didn't smile back. "Oh, he asked if he could add an appendix onto the end of the list. I asked him why he couldn't put it on the emergency list, but he said that as he was available now, it would be easier. He won't listen when I told him that there weren't enough staff, that everybody was going off duty, but he insists on it being done now. So, it means that everybody is going to be late off, not only me and the anaesthetist, just because he doesn't want to have to come back, after the plastic surgeons have done some cases."
"You do know that the list in theatre three is still going on, and the rest of the late staff are on that list?" Bella asked, and Katrina nodded. "So, who's going to scrub for the appendix?" she added, and Katrina looked at her friend. "Who else?" she said. "I'm going to have to stay on. I'm just hoping he gets a bit of a shift on, and I don't have to stay too late."
"I'll stay if you want me to" Bella offered, but Katrina shook her head. "No, you go home. You said you were going out with Tom tonight and you don't want to be late for him, do you?"
"Are you going out tonight?" Bella asked. "I thought that you had something to do on a Monday evening?"
"I do normally. I'm going to rehearsal, but as I only wanted to verify some measurements, it won't hurt

if I'm late." She grinned at her deputy. "I've got to make a dress for the dame, and I need to get a pattern, so, as I don't want to get one that's the wrong size, I've got to measure him and get his vital statistics."

"Who's playing the dame this year?" Bella grinned. She had heard plenty about the dramatic society that Katrina was involved with, as the wardrobe mistress, altering existing costumes, or making new ones, and knew some of the people involved. "Keith Jenkins." Katrina said, and the two girls grinned widely. Keith was one of the orthopaedic surgeons in their hospital, and was a larger-than-life character, tall, broad of shoulder, but with a devil may care charm. He was well liked by everybody, and he thoroughly enjoyed acting in pantomimes, normally as the Dame. "Oh well, I'd better go and get a quick drink before I have to scrub" she said now. "I left Elaine and Sue finishing the last case, so hopefully I'll be ready before Dr. Summers gets the patient here. Elaine is off at five, Sue isn't off until six, but as she's just finishing the last case, I said I'd scrub, so she can have a break. Blasted man" she growled again, then smiled. "Go when it's time Bella, and I'll see you tomorrow." Bella nodded, and watched as Katrina went quickly to the coffee room, to make herself a drink. The surgeon in question, Simon Parker, was new to the department, and got on well with everybody, apart from Katrina Howarth, the senior sister. There was always an odd atmosphere around, but nobody knew why. Maybe it was just one of those things, where two people had an immediate bad reaction to each other. Bella sighed and finished what she was doing, and as the clock ticked round to five, she made ready to leave. She said her goodbyes to the other girls, and walked away to get changed. At least Mr. Parker wasn't operating tomorrow, so Katrina might be in a better mood, she thought as she changed her clothes and left the department.

Katrina sipped her drink in the coffee room, still annoyed at the way Mr. Parker had got his own way. They just didn't have enough staff to run three theatres after five, when most of the staff went home, but he couldn't seem to understand that, expecting the staff to stay on, and work. She got up and went into the laying up room, to get some instruments ready for the case. She was tall, well built, with deep brown eyes, long dark auburn hair, hidden now under a theatre cap, and pulled back from her face, and her mother had often remarked that she had a temper to match her hair colour, but she was able to keep it in check, most of the time. She could see Elaine and Sue making sure that their patient was fit enough to be moved to the recovery room, and the student nurse was busy clearing up, for the theatre looked a mess at the moment. Rebecca, the student was doing very well, she thought to herself. She liked theatre work, and had expressed an interest in returning when she was qualified, and hoped that the girl would pass her exams and there would be enough money to be able to employ her. This was her last week of working in the theatres, and after that, no more students had been allocated. Trying to get the committee to authorise the money to be able to appoint new staff was a nightmare recently! Now, she got the set of instruments ready, made sure that there was nothing missing and after letting Rebecca know that she was going to scrub, went away to do so. When she returned clad in a theatre gown, hands covered in sterile gloves, and her face hidden by the mask she had tied on, so that only her eyes showed, she was able to prepare the trolley, to make sure that all her instruments were correct, and she was ready to get on with the operation. The previous patient had gone, the theatre was clean and tidy, and she was just about to push the trolley into the theatre, when Simon Parker appeared in the doorway. He seemed to tower over everything and everybody, but he was broad with it, His hair, like hers was dark auburn, but cut short, and he had deep blue eyes. "Do we have the laparoscopy instruments available?" he asked curtly, and Katrina nodded. "Everything's ready" she said. "This isn't going to take too long, I hope"

"Why, got a date?" he asked, and grinned at her. She was on the verge of denying that, when she saw the grin, and changed her mind. "Yes," she said quietly, "and he's not going to be too pleased if I'm late. I'm allowing you to do this case, only because the patient is so ill, but this is it. If you have an emergency after your next list, it goes on the emergency list, and you'll have to negotiate its urgency with the other surgeons. We simply don't have enough staff to run three theatres after five o clock. Overtime isn't paid, for nurses you know?"

"But you can take time back in lieu, can't you?" he asked, his eyes narrowing, but Katrina gave a hollow laugh. "When do we ever get the opportunity to take time back? As I said, we sometimes don't have enough staff to cope with the lists, let alone allow us to take time back" she said, then looked past him to see the patient being wheeled into theatre. "Your patient is here" she said, and he turned away, to see the patient being placed on the operating table, to go and get him ready for surgery.

Over an hour later, she was still stood at the table, handing instruments with her usual skill, as Simon Parker peered at the screen, which he had been doing since the start of the operation. "This is definitely not an appendix" he announced, "but I can't see what's causing the problem. We're going to have to open him up, and investigate. Sorry everybody, somebody made a big mistake in diagnosing this as an appendix."
The anaesthetist had looked at Katrina as he said that, and raised his eyebrows, and Katrina knew that something was going to be said by him to his colleagues. The anaesthetic nurse, Sarah, should have been off duty at the same time at Katrina, but had offered to stay for a while, and for the last few minutes had been taking a message from the anaesthetist, who had asked her to phone home to let his wife know that he was going to be very late. Now, she beckoned Sarah to her. "When you've phoned Dr. Steven's wife, to let her know what's happening, nip into Theatre three, and find out what they are up to, and ask them to come and take over as soon as they can." she murmured, and Sarah nodded and went out of the room. Simon Parker looked at Katrina. "My apologies Sister. I hope this

won't cause problems with your date."
Katrina glared at him. "I think you need to apologise to Sarah when she gets back into theatre" she said. "She only agreed to stay because she was assured that this would be a very quick case, and as she has childcare issues, she is the person who needs to be relieved as soon as possible. My personal life isn't that much of a problem."
"Who did you have a date with Katrina?" The person asking the question was Simon's registrar, Joe, whose wife was a long-time friend of Katrina, but she glared at him, and he looked away.
"Joe, my private life is my own affair, as you well know" she said quietly, and he nodded. "Sorry" he muttered, and turned his attention back to the operation site. Doctor Stevens looked across at Simon. "Who told you this was an appendix, Simon?" he asked. "Nobody on your team I hope?"
"No, it was James Hall, from Ewan Dexter's team. He assured me it was definitely an appendix and wouldn't take more than five minutes to whip it out. There was no reason to suspect it would be anything else. No medical history of anything else."
"Not like James to make a mistake like that" Doctor Stevens growled, and looked up, as Sarah came back into the theatre, and walked to where Katrina was stood, and murmured the bad news to her. "Sorry Katrina, theatre three is still working, and they don't look as though they're going to finish any time soon. I did tell everybody that you needed relief, and they've promised to come over as soon as they finish the case. However, Hayley from Neuro is coming to relieve me. Dawn phoned while I was outside and

asked for the situation, and she's sending her up. Brenda said that as soon as she finishes her case on the emergency list, she'll close that theatre and get the staff in here, so you can go home, but the one they're doing, looks like it could go on for hours." Katrina nodded her thanks, and Sarah went back to stand beside Doctor Stevens. She was getting some more equipment ready for the doctor, for the patient had only been given a short anaesthetic, and as it now appeared, the operation was going to take a lot longer, more drugs needed to be injected, and preparations made for a longer operation. The door behind her opened and Hayley, the anaesthetic nurse from Neuro theatre entered, and the two girls had a quick hand over, before Sarah made her farewells, and left the theatre. Katrina had sent Sue home, and she was left with Rebecca, the student nurse, but she was not worried for the student nurse was calm and relaxed, and would make a good scrub nurse if she was able to return to theatres.

It was nearly nine thirty when Katrina finally managed to get off duty. The operation had taken a long time to complete, and had been much more complex than envisaged, requiring lots of different instruments, and more surgical staff needed to be called to assist. The patient had displayed signs of an appendix, but in fact the problem had been arterial, and needed an aneurysm, a ballooning of the main artery, the aorta, to be repaired, and they had almost lost the patient when it had burst, but they had saved his life, and he should now recover and be able to live a fuller life. However, none of the other staff had been able to relieve her, for the staff in the other theatres were also having problems. Brenda had appeared in the doorway of the theatre and asked her if she wanted relief when they were just putting in the first layer of sutures, and she had summoned up a tired grin, and refused. "You can help Rebecca clean the theatre when we're finished, if you wouldn't mind" she said, "I'll get the list of implants together and the night staff can order them and do the rest of the ordering at the same time. We're almost finished now in any case, so I'll do a final swab check if you wouldn't mind, Rebecca." The young girl had counted swabs with her, and with a sigh, she got down from her platform, pushed the trolleys away from the table, and took the dressing from the student nurse, and applied it to the patient's abdomen. "Thank you, Sister" Simon Parker said, as she prepared to fill in the paperwork that went with the case, before Hayley could accompany the patient to the intensive care unit. "I apologise once more for the misunderstanding."

"Try not to let it happen again" she said coldly, gave Hayley the papers she had completed, and walked to the office. She put the list of implants they had used on the desk, in the clip where the night staff could see them, entered her overtime in the book, and walked to theatre three to see how they were getting on. The patient on the table was still undergoing surgery, and she glanced at the operating book as she walked past it. The time the operation started showed that it hadn't begun until gone 7.00 pm, and she could have been relieved by the theatre staff, had they stopped the list. She had not given permission for the list to run on, especially as she had been due to go off duty two hours previous to that time. The theatre was silent, as she stared at the surgeon but he refused to meet her gaze, and dropped his eyes to his patient. "Who sent for the patient?" she demanded, and he remarked blithely, "I did." Katrina drew in a deep calming breath before she said "I would like to see you in my office tomorrow Mr. James", and there was a sudden quiet in the theatre. Everybody in the theatre knew there was going to be trouble tomorrow, and Katrina knew also, she was going to have a problem with the surgeon. "Good night girls" she announced and left the theatre, and stamped into the changing room, where she tore out of her theatre outfit and into her outdoor clothes. She grabbed her coat and handbag, trod into her shoes and went into the coffee room to get her bag. The silence as she went in, showed the surgeons had been talking about her, and she gave them a curt nod. "Goodnight" she said and walked out of the unit. She was tired and hungry, she'd been on duty since 8.00 am that morning, she hadn't eaten anything, since a biscuit at 4.00 pm, and she wasn't looking forward to the following day, and knew that she was going to have to involve the nursing officer in the argument that was bound to take place with Mr. James on the following day. "How dare he" she muttered to herself, as she walked out of the hospital, towards the block of flats where she lived. All the staff in that theatre had known that she had had to stay late to assist Simon Parker, but she wasn't going to blame her nursing staff for not finishing the list. Darren James was well known for sending for the next patient despite a lack of staff, and she was disgusted with him. He had no consideration for anybody else at all, and she was going to have to get support from the nursing officer the next day. Wearily she entered the building where she lived and walked up the flight of steps to her front door. She wasn't going to go to rehearsal now, it would nearly be finished anyway, and she knew she would be able to get her measurements at some other time. She opened the front door of the flat, and entered, picking up the post as she did so – a postcard from her mother, and a letter from her sister. She took them into the kitchen, and opened the fridge door. She wasn't going to cook anything, she thought, she was too tired, and instead filled the kettle, and while waiting for it to boil, took the loaf of bread from the bin, and cut off a couple of thick slices, spreading them with butter and marmite, while she read the postcard. Her parents were away on a cruise, fulfilling an ambition they had cherished for a long time, and she didn't know when they would return. Her sister's letter, she decided to leave unopened until she had made the tea, so she could concentrate on its contents. Her sister, in fact her twin, Eleanor, was a doctor in a hospital in London. They didn't get to meet very often, for Eleanor’s work as a senior house officer was unpredictable, were frequently unable to speak to each other at a time when they weren't working, so kept in touch by e mails and letters. The kettle boiled and she made a pot of tea, and took it into the sitting room to eat her bread and butter, drink her tea, and finally open Eleanor's letter.

Eleanor had trained, and still worked at St. Anselm's, and Katrina had been doing her nurse training at the same hospital, so the two girls had many shared friends, and Katrina enjoyed reading about people she had known until she had moved away. In fact, the first time she had met Simon Parker had been when he had worked at St. Anselm's, and they had encountered each other when she had been a student working on the wards. He hadn't taken any notice of her, but she had known who he was, and before he arrived, had wondered whether he had improved since he worked at her training hospital and come to work at Queens where she now ran the theatre unit. She had known that Eleanor had met him, but they had never encountered him when they were together, and he wondered if he knew that they were twins. He had never acknowledged that they had met previously, when he had turned up as the newest consultant in the department where she was now working. Now, she read her sisters letter, laughing at some of the comments, then stared astounded as the last paragraph. In it, her sister mentioned she was coming to work at Queens hospital, and the two of them would be reunited for a while. She read the last few lines again, *"I applied for, and managed to win a scholarship to do more arterial work, so Katy dear, I'll be working for a Mr. Parker, and then a Mr. Dexter. What are they like? Hope they're going to be good to a junior doctor who only wants to learn how they do certain surgeries. Write soon and let me know won't you. I don't know the date when I'll be arriving yet, but I'll be getting accommodation in the doctor quarters, so I won't be scrounging for a bed, but we'll be able to see each other quite frequently. And you never know, I'll be in theatre, occasionally, when they are operating, and you might be the scrub nurse for operations, and I'll be able to give you some menial jobs to do! Just joking Katy, but I'm so looking forward to seeing you again."* Katrina smiled widely at the thought of meeting her sister again, and working with her, and determined to write the following evening, when she was off duty. She wondered how much Eleanor would be learning from Simon Parker and Ewan Dexter, and how long the scholarship would last. She sighed, finished her tea and went to have a swift bath, before going to her bed.

The next morning, she allocated staff to theatres for operations that day, told Bella about the previous evening, and phoned her nursing officer for an appointment, which was granted for later on in the morning. When she talked to the older woman, she was reassured that the problems were known about, and other people had complained about the situation, mostly the anaesthetic staff who were affected as well. While Katrina was with her, Miss Betts phoned the anaesthetic department and asked if Doctor Davidson, the anaesthetist who had been working with Mr. James the previous night, could come and see her now, and when the man arrived, discussed the problems they had been having. Luckily Doctor Ian Davidson was very understanding, and knew very well, what the problems were. "I wasn't aware that there weren't enough people,

Sister" he said now to Katrina. "I did query if there were enough staff, but Darren James assured me that there were. I would never have allowed him to send for the patient if I'd known that the early staff had been required to stay on to do another case."
"Why didn't you ask any of the nursing staff? They were all aware that I had been required to stay late." Katrina said quietly, and the nursing officer shot her a glance. "I did ask Staff Nurse Ellison, but Darren answered. I wondered if she'd heard me asking her."
"Probably not" Katrina said. "Staff Nurse Ellison has to wear hearing aids, as you probably know, so she would have been concentrating on what Mr. James wanted, and not listening to anybody else. If she had heard the question, there is no way she would have given permission for you to send for the case in question. And anyway, Mr. James list is meant to finish at 5.00 pm, and he simply cannot be allowed to book cases that run into the evening, as he seems to take delight in doing. Luckily, I was not doing anything important last night, but I had been working since 8.00 am, and working a 13-hour day is not what I signed up to do. Especially as we don't get paid for overtime, as you are well aware."
Ian Davidson looked a bit taken back at her comment, and slightly guilty as well. He was not on the hospital committee, that had over-ruled the nursing officer's requests that the nurses should be paid overtime, as they were unable to take time back, but he was the liaison person, and did have some input to the committee, and Katrina hoped that he would feel some guilt about it. "Well, I'm sure you can be paid for last night's overtime" he

said with a smile, but she didn't smile back. "That's not the point. We simply don't have enough staff" she said now. "We have told the committee several times, we don't have enough personnel, especially as we are getting busier, but nobody listens to us. We are five people down already in general theatres, and the other theatres are in a similar situation, but we still aren't being allowed to advertise for more personnel."

"It's true Ian." Miss Betts broke in. "I've told you on more than one occasion that we need more staff, but my comments are always ignored. If this is going to happen more often, as I can see that it will do, I am not going to allow my staff to be overworked in this manner. If we don't get more staff, then I can see that I am going to have to make some executive decisions, and refuse to allow surgeons to put more than two large cases onto their operating lists."

"You can't do that" the anaesthetist said angrily, but the nursing office had the bit between her teeth now, and Katrina knew that this was a pivotal moment in the meeting. "I can do that and I will continue to do so, unless more staff are appointed. Sister Howarth and the sisters in the other theatres are doing a sterling job allowing the surgeons to do as many operations as is possible, but all their staff are all working at their full capacity, and need assistance. I notice that there isn't a block on the number of medical staff being appointed, apparently two or three of the consultants are getting more house officers – it's just the nursing staff whose numbers are restricted, and after discussing the case with the other nursing officers, I hear that it's only theatres that are affected. The wards do seem to be getting extra people now. I will be requesting a full meeting of the committee unless something is done." Ian Davidson gave in. He knew that everything she had said was true, and that the committee had put a cap on the number of theatre nursing staff to be appointed, but he hadn't done anything about it. "I'll talk to them, and put in a full written report" he promised. "I didn't realise exactly how bad the situation was. Something will have to be done, but you know what they are like trying to save money."

"Would they prefer to appoint more staff, or have to pay out in legal fees when the nurses make mistakes because they are overworked and tired?" Miss Betts asked, and he nodded. "Leave it with me. I promise that something will be done, and done soon." he added, then smiled at the two women. "In the meantime, what are we going to do about Darren James? He's the one who caused this upset, and he needs to be told exactly what problems he's caused."

"I asked to see him in the theatre office this morning" Katrina said softly, and then grinned. "But If we were all to go to his office, and have a chat with him, maybe he'd realise the seriousness of the situation, and bring home to him just what he caused last night." Ian Davidson nodded. "Sounds good to me" he agreed. "I'll make sure he's available, if I might use your phone?" he asked Miss Betts, who nodded. There was a short conversation, before he replaced the receiver, and said, "He's there now. No time like the present" he said, and the three of them walked to the consultant's office.

An hour later, Katrina returned to the theatre block, and sank down in her seat in the office. She was staring at some paperwork, and looked up as Bella came in and shut the door behind her. "What happened?" she asked, "Did he apologise?"
"Oh, he apologised alright" Katrina laughed. "He couldn't do anything other than apologise, with Mr. Davidson and Miss Betts present as well. He has agreed that his lists will be shorter, and that before he sends for another case, he will consult with the senior nurse present, and will make sure that there are enough staff on duty for him to do the case he wants to do. However, you haven't heard the best bit yet – Miss Betts managed to 'persuade' Dr. Davidson to discuss things with the committee, and hopefully, we're to be allowed to recruit more staff – both anaesthetic and scrub, which means that we might be able to keep Rebecca if she qualifies and wants a job. He wasn't too happy at being asked, citing monetary problems, but she pointed out that it would cost them more if patients suffered due to mistakes made by nurses because they were tired."
Bella grinned at the explanation. "So, for the next few weeks, everybody is going to be well behaved, and ask permission from you or I before they send for another patient, but then they'll 'forget', and the early staff will have to stay over time again, and the situation will be as bad as it is now."
"Don't be such a cynic" Katrina said, but she knew that her friend spoke the truth. "We'll have to make sure that if we tell them no, we mean it. It will be the

junior medical staff we'll have to tell first, and I've got a secret weapon up my sleeve about that" and she told Bella that her sister would be coming to work with Simon Parker and Ewan Dexter. Bella grinned. "I'm going to look forward to her coming" she said now, "Are you identical?" Bella asked, but Katrina shook her head. "No, I don't think we look anything like each other. Our only similarity is our eyes, we've both got the same shape eyes, and mum once said that when we're wearing a mask, when we both dressed as theatre nurses for a fancy-dress party, she couldn't tell the difference between us. I don't believe that, because I'm taller than she is, and I weigh more than she does. But Bella, please don't tell anybody else. This could be fun."
Bella nodded, "Why don't you go and get yourself a drink, unless you had one with Miss Betts?" she said now. "We've all had a drink, apart from the girls who are scrubbed, and then we've got enough staff to cope until lunchtime. You could get on with the paperwork, before we'll need you this afternoon. Emily is on a half day, so we'll be a body light, and we're going to need you in one of the theatres." Katrina nodded, and Bella went back to the theatre where she had been working.

Katrina had made herself a drink, and taken it back to the office, where she was wrestling with the off duty, when there was a tap at the door, and without looking up, she called "come in", and was surprised when she encountered Simon Parker's gaze. "Hello Mr. Parker" she said politely, "what can I do for you?"

"I wanted to apologise for last night's problems." he said slowly. "I didn't realise how few staff you had on duty last night. Did it cause you any problems on a personal level, because I understand you had to cancel a date because of it?"
"No," Katrina answered, "not really, but that's beside the point. Situations like that shouldn't happen, and I hope in future you'll understand when I refuse to let you send for another patient, even if it is going to be for a small operation." He nodded, then spoke again. "It shouldn't have been diagnosed as an appendix either, and I've already spoken to the house officer about the fact that he managed make a mistake like that. Especially when it turned out to be an aortic aneurysm without any history of illness. But I'm sure you would agree that there was a great deal of urgency for the case to be done. You could see that for yourself couldn't you?
"Yes, I quite agree that the surgery was urgent, and in a case like that, then the nursing staff would do all they could to assist in saving a patient's life, but might I remind you Mr. Parker, that you 'just' wanted to operate on a supposed appendix, because you were in theatre already and didn't want to have to return when there was space on the emergency list."
He nodded, "And I apologise for that as well. The patient is doing quite well, incidentally. Just thought I'd let you know."
"Thank you" Katrina said gratefully, and Simon hesitated before he spoke again. "The house officers will be changing in three weeks' time. I hope that the person who replaces James Hall won't make such a pig's ear of the diagnosis as James did last night."

"Do you know who is going to replace him?" she asked, as she took a sip of her drink, but Simon shook his head. "It's a female, who comes from St. Anselm's. She's won a scholarship to work with me, and with Ewan Dexter, because she wants to get more experience of arterial work, so she's taking the place of one of the house officers. Hope to goodness it's not one of the dippy females who I worked with when I was there. Even some of the nurses I worked with were the same type." Katrina drew in a deep breath, and refused to rise to the bait. "I'm sure that this woman, whoever she is, will prove to be quite good." she answered, and abruptly Simon stood up. "Do you know what is on your list for tomorrow yet Mr. Parker?" Katrina asked, and to her astonishment, he grinned. "Yes," he replied "I've got a list somewhere, but I've left it in the office. I'll make sure you get to see it very soon, and you'll be able to cut it down to a manageable level. I've just read an e mail from Ian Davidson" he added, and suddenly Katrina realised that the anaesthetist had contacted all the surgeons and let them know what had been decided. "I'll look forward to reading it." she said quietly, and watched as he left the office.

When she got home that evening, she made herself a meal, for she was quite hungry, then sat down with her writing pad to inform her sister about the two men she would be working for, and by the time the letter was finished and ready to post, she was tired. She knew she would be seeing Keith Jenkins the following day, and as she still needed to verify his measurements, she placed her long tape measure in her bag, in case she had an opportunity to use it on the surgeon, before making herself a final drink, and went to bed.

Chapter Two

Three weeks later, Katrina plumped up the cushions on the settee, and made sure that the tea tray was ready in the kitchen, ready for her visitors. It was going to be a great occasion, for Eleanor, plus David and James, their brothers, were also going to be visiting. Their eldest brother, David, was also a doctor, a medical consultant, working at a hospital about 10 miles away from Queens, and James, was a senior paramedic. For them all to have the same weekend off, was an unusual occurrence, and consequently they were going to celebrate being able to get together. Now, she was just waiting for the rest of her family to arrive, and soon, the doorbell rang and she eagerly went to open it. David was waiting there and she embraced him eagerly, hugging and kissing him in welcome. They hadn't been able to meet for a few months, although they kept in contact regularly, so they had a lot of news to catch up on. They were exchanging news, when the doorbell rang again, and James was on the doorstep. Ten minutes later, Eleanor arrived, and all the siblings were together, exchanging news and gossip. Naturally enough, some of the talk was about Eleanor's new job, and who she would be working for. "I'm going to be senior house officer to Simon Parker and Ewan Dexter" she said now, and David looked interested. "I was in the same year at med. School as Simon Parker. We lost contact after we qualified. Can you say hello to him for me?" he said. "How's he doing now?"
"Oh, he's not too bad" Katrina said, "he's the senior

consultant in arterial work, and thank goodness he's not a RLGA (Right Little God Almighty). He did come and apologise to me for making me work overtime a few weeks ago. One of the other surgeons, who always runs over, had got the late staff in his theatre, but although he said he asked them if it was okay to send for another patient, he obviously didn't. The emergency list was going on, and as we don't have three teams of nurses available, guess who had to stay on and do a 13-hour day, because he wanted to add a seriously ill appendix, which turned out to be an aortic aneurysm, onto the end of his list? That was a serious case of mis-diagnosis, I can tell you, and the doctor who did it, is the one that Elly is replacing." She drew in a deep breath, "I'm hoping Elly, that if he wants to add patients onto the list, and I tell you we don't have enough staff, that you're going to tell him that he's not going to be able to do the operation." Her sister grinned at her. "I might do, but there again, I might not." David looked at her sternly, "No," he said, "you won't. If you do that, you're going to get a reputation for being somebody who doesn't listen to the theatre staff, and they won't want to work with you."
"Oh David" Eleanor said softly, "I wouldn't do that, but I would have to try and please my boss wouldn't I?"
"Yes," he nodded, "but just remember who is in charge of the theatres, and obey everything that she says to you." He grinned at Katrina. "I'm sure that Eleanor will listen to you, and obey everything you say, but if she doesn't just let me know and I'll come and give her a good hiding."

"You wouldn't" Eleanor gasped, and didn't see the wink that David gave to Katrina.

"Yes, I would" he answered, "the theatre staff need their time off, just as you do, and if you had to stay that late, you'd be complaining, wouldn't you?" Eleanor nodded and knew that her older brother meant what he said. "Have the surgeons been better behaved lately?" James asked and Katrina nodded. "I don't know how long it's going to last, but the senior nurses are being asked if it's okay to send for another patient, and the consultants aren't objecting if we say that they can't. It's been quite good actually, but I don't think it will continue." David looked at her closely. "You look tired." he said, "Is everything okay with the department now?" he asked and she nodded. "It's not too bad" she said, "but if the promised new staff don't arrive, then things could go downhill again. I think Dr. Davidson got quite a shock, when Miss Betts told him that she was going to restrict the surgeons to two large cases per day, if he didn't persuade the committee to allow some more staff to be recruited." David laughed and changed the subject. Katrina had produced a meal for her siblings, and they were sitting around the table, having eaten, when James asked his sisters "What about your love life? Anybody on the horizon?" Katrina had shaken her head, and grinned at her brother. He was happily married and his wife who was also a nurse, had just announced that she was expecting their first baby in six months' time, and he wanted his sisters to be happy as he was. "I don't meet anybody apart from surgeons, and I don't think I'd want to marry one of them. Now, a medic

would be okay, I expect" David shook his head. "No, I don't think so." he answered. "We don't seem to have any more free time than the surgical team do. At least if you married a surgeon, you'd see him occasionally, when he came to theatre. What about you, Elly? Anybody in view?" Eleanor smiled at him, and lowered her eye lids to her plate. "Wouldn't you like to know?" she said, then grinned at her brothers. "I've been out with a couple of guys from St. Anselm's, but as I'm going to be working here for the next six months, they might lose interest."
"If they really like you they won't." David said. "What about you?" Katrina asked, but David shook his head. "Nobody special" he replied evasively, then turned the talk to other matters. The two men had to leave before it became too late, and Katrina and Eleanor said goodbye to her brothers, hoping they would be able to see each other again soon. The sisters were left together, and the two girls smiled at each other. "It is good to see you again" Katrina said softly. "I'm really looking forward to working with you. Nobody knows we're sisters, apart from one of my staff nurses, but she's promised to keep that a secret, so we might be able to surprise everybody at the end of your placement, by announcing it. Of course, the different names will help." She was referring to the fact that when they had started training, and David had been working at the same hospital, it had been decided that to have two doctor Howarth's would be confusing, so Eleanor had changed her surname to Howard, so the sisters had different surnames. Eleanor looked at her sister. "I'd better go" she said. "I'm due to start at

7.30 tomorrow morning, and I need to be on duty bright and early, so I ought to get some sleep. I've moved into the doctor's house already, but I'll phone you, and we can go for a drink together,"
"Or you could come round for a meal" Katrina finished her sister's sentence, and the girls grinned at each other. "Just be nice to me" Eleanor said, and Katrina grinned. "Aren't I always nice to you?" she asked, before bidding her sister goodnight.

The following day, Katrina went into work, wondering when her sister would come into theatre. The day wore on, and it was the end of the afternoon, and they had finished Simon's list, before she came to the unit and he introduced her to Katrina. As they were introduced, Katrina could see that Eleanor was hiding laughter, but managed to keep a straight face, as they shook hands. "Welcome to the department" she said. "Come with me and I'll take you round and show you where you can get changed." and she escorted her out of the room. "Changing room" she said, "The code for the door is this" and she gave her the letters and numbers to be entered on the key pad. She escorted her sister around the department, telling her where things were located, and introducing her to various members of the nursing staff. At the end of the tour, she took her into the coffee room, and they found Simon Parker waiting for them. "We've got an emergency to book" he said. "I've been told it's an appendix, so we can get it done now as the list ended early."
"No, we can't" Katrina said firmly. "I've told you

before Mr. Parker, you should put the details on the emergency list, or if it's very urgent, liaise with the other surgeons to get it done quicker. The list is not going to over-run again. We have had this discussion before, if you remember, and unless its life or death, then the operation will not be done at the end of your list. On the other hand, if you want to discuss things with Mr. James, then he might allow you to do your case, but there are simply not enough staff to run three lists after 5.00pm." Simon Parker looked annoyed and raised his eyes to heaven. Eleanor said softly, "Well, why can't you open another theatre, Sister?" and Katrina gave her sister an annoyed glance. "Weren't you listening?" she said, "Because we don't have enough staff" she said quietly. "I have four nurses on duty after five pm, along with one auxiliary nurse. There are two nurses per theatre, plus one auxiliary between the two theatres, which is one short of the minimum number of staff needed, and those nurses are doing Mr. James list which is over-running, as usual, and the emergency list which has just started."

"Well, why can't you stay and do the operation?" Eleanor asked, and Katrina's eyes opened wide with annoyance at her sister. "Because I am off duty in five minutes, I do not have any anaesthetic staff who are willing to stay late, I have an appointment tonight, which I am not going to miss yet again, and I do not get paid for overtime. I'm sorry, but you are new to the department, and I must ask you not to interfere with the way I run the theatres."

Simon nodded. "It would be better if we could get the patient operated on, early" he said, but Katrina gave him a hard look. “Don't push it Mr. Parker” she said coldly, “Go and talk to Mr. James. Now, I am going off duty, when I've talked to my other staff. Goodnight” and she walked away, wondering as she did so, what Eleanor thought she was about. She checked with the other nurses on duty that things were satisfactory. “There's an appendix that Simon Parker wants to do” she muttered to the nurse doing the emergency list. “I've refused him permission to do it on the end of his list, so he's going to talk to Darren James, but he's going to want to do it soon. I'm going off now, because I'm determined he's not going to make me stay on duty again. I'll see you tomorrow.”

“Okay Katrina. See you tomorrow.” Anne, the staff nurse in charge of theatres that night, smiled and watched as Katrina walked away.

When she reached home that evening, and was cooking herself a meal, the way her sister had tried to get her to stay on duty came back to her, and she shook her head. She didn't know how to react. She had told Eleanor the problems, when David and James had been present, and David had told her to behave so differently than she had done. He had threatened to tell her off, and although he had been joking, Eleanor didn't know that, and wondered whether or not she was going to have to get her brother involved. She decided that if it happened again, then she would have to contact David and get his advice. She suddenly remembered another occasion when the two girls were a lot younger, and Eleanor had deliberately done something that her parent's had forbidden her to do, and got her into trouble, when she had lied and told them that it was Katrina, who had done it. Her father had been very angry with her, but had apologised to her, when she had been able to convince her mother that it hadn't been her fault, and she had passed the information to her husband. There had been other occasions as well, but normally the two girls had a good relationship. Deciding that she could do nothing, until she had a chance to talk to her sister, she gathered everything she would need for fitting costumes, and went to rehearsal. When she reached the rehearsal rooms, she was delighted to find that all her costumes fitted the people they were intended for, and nothing major needed to be done. She gathered everything together, said her farewells to the cast of the pantomime, and went home.

The following day she went into work, took the report from the night nurses, and discovered that the appendix had been done on the emergency list about 30 minutes after she had left. Anne gave her the news that Mr. Parker had done the operation in thirty minutes, and the patient had been back on the ward later that evening. "So, what did you think of his new senior house officer?" Katrina asked, and was surprised when Anne shook her head. "We're going to have problems with that one" she said quietly. "She was throwing her weight about, trying to make us all look stupid, when she didn't really know what she was doing herself. I think Mr. Parker was amused by it. She's obviously attracted to him as well, and is trying to make sure he knows where she is, and what she's doing. It could be quite funny to watch. But maybe somebody needs to talk to her, and let her know that the theatre staff are all highly qualified nurses, and we shouldn't be treated like idiots."

"Well, if she does it to me, I'll definitely take her to one side, and give her some instruction."

She smiled at her staff nurse. "Don't you remember one of the SHO's we had a couple of years ago, didn't realise that nurses know what they are doing, and tried to treat us like idiots. But he soon learnt, didn't he? It didn't take long to make him understand that he shouldn't treat us like complete fools. If necessary, I'll talk to her. But apart from that, anything else happen?"

"No," said Anne. "We managed to finish the list and we all got off duty on time. Nice easy evening, really." Katrina smiled. "Thank goodness." she said "Have we got enough staff for the lists today?"

"If you can scrub for the dental list, then yes, we have. But we don't have enough people to have two on that list, so you'd have to do the list on your own."

"That's okay. I can get that list done quite easily. Is everybody else, okay?" Anne nodded. "We'll be fine this afternoon" she said, "and hopefully somebody can replace you if necessary."

"That won't be necessary" Katrina said, looking at the dental list she was going to scrub for. "We should be finished this list by lunchtime, and then I can get into the office this afternoon." she grinned. "I'll go and get the sets out, then come and have a quick drink and hopefully see you later." The two girls parted, and got on with their day's work.

Two weeks later, Katrina had again done the dental list in the morning, on her own, before going into the office to catch up on some paperwork. Simon Parker had not put a foot out of line since Eleanor's arrival, but that afternoon, as Katrina sat in the office, doing some of the paperwork, she was interrupted by Eleanor who came into the office. "Hi Katy" she said as she came in. "I've bought Mr. Parker's list for tomorrow for you to see." Katrina took the list and glanced at it. "No way" she said now, "There won't be enough time to get all these cases done. I suggest that he comes and talk to me and we can decide which cases he thinks are the most urgent."

"All of them" Eleanor said. "He wants to get all of them done tomorrow."

"Well, he's not going to get them all done." Katrina said firmly. "Sorry Eleanor, I need to talk to him, before the list starts tomorrow."

"I'll tell him, but he's a bit busy at the moment, and I think he said he's going out tonight, so he won't be available."

"Well, if he doesn't come and talk to me, I'm cancelling the last four on the list now, and I shall contact the ward sisters and tell them to feed the patients, because they won't get done. Miss Betts did tell all the surgeons that they could only put two large cases per day on the list, but he's got seven on this list."

"Aren't you taking a bit too much on yourself?" Eleanor said, and Katrina gave her sister a long hard look. “No,” she replied, “I am not. I am in charge of this department, and the lists are my responsibility. Go and find Mr. Parker, and tell him what I've said. And do it now, because otherwise, I will cancel some of the cases.” and she turned her attention back to the paper she was studying. Eleanor got up to go and Katrina spoke as her sister reached the door. “And Eleanor, if I hear that you are trying to throw your weight about as you did that first night you worked, then I will be talking to David. Remember what he said when we were having dinner?” and she looked back at the papers. Eleanor muttered something which sounded like “you're no fun anymore” as she walked out, and Katrina drew in a deep breath. She didn't want to get on bad terms with her sister, but she couldn't allow her to cause problems in the department. She had gone to see if everybody was coping, and from there to the coffee room to have a drink, when Simon Parker came in to the room. “What's the problem Katrina?” he asked. “Dr Howard said you needed to speak to me.”

“Yes,” Katrina said. “She showed me the list for tomorrow. We are going to have to cut it down because there is no way you are going to get all those cases done. Who do you want to cancel now, or do you want to put them straight onto the emergency list?”

“I've only got three cases tomorrow” he said with surprise. “They are fairly big ones, but I have doubts that I’ll overrun. There's a gastrectomy, the aneurysm and a laparotomy which is probably going to end in another gastrectomy, which shouldn’t take too long.”

"The list I saw had two aneurysms and five laparotomies on it." Katrina said. "It's in the office. Come and have a look at it, and see why I said I needed to see you."

They went along to the office together and Katrina picked up the list that was lying on the desk, and handed it to the surgeon. He read it, and looked up. "This is nonsense. This bears no resemblance to the list I would like to do" he said. "Who bought it to you?"

"Your SHO, Eleanor Howard." she answered, but he shook his head. "This isn't the list I asked her to bring to you." He grinned at her. "I think she's trying to wind you up. I operated on a couple of these patients a week or so ago, and they're being discharged soon. In fact, that aneurysm patient, is the one that you stayed late to do."

"I thought the name was familiar" Katrina muttered, then "Well Dr. Howard succeeded in winding me up. "Do you have a copy of the list you actually do want to do?" He nodded and produced a sheet of paper. "If you have a look at that, I'll leave it with you. Who will be scrubbing?" She shook her head. "I haven't done the work list yet, so I don't know."

"Would you be able to scrub if necessary?" he asked. "I'd like you to scrub for the aneurysm, if possible, because I need a very good, very experienced scrub nurse." He smiled at her, and she smiled back. "I don't see why not" she said, looking at the number of staff on duty, and was surprised when he hesitated, then spoke. "Do you fancy going out for a drink tonight?" She looked at him, shocked then remembered Eleanor's words. "I thought you were

going out tonight" she said, and he looked at her quizzically. "Who told you that?" he asked.
"Eleanor Howard" she replied. "She said you wouldn't be able to talk to me about the list because you were busy this afternoon, and you were going out this evening."
"Don't know where she got that idea from" he said. "I was working in my office this afternoon, until she mentioned in passing, that you wanted to see me, and I certainly haven't told her what I'm doing this evening. But what about it? Do you fancy having a drink? We could go to the Crown, if you would like to. It's never too busy there, and we could have a chat."
Katrina thought for a while, then smiled at him. "Okay" she said. "What time do you want to meet?" he grinned at her. "Eight suit you?" he asked and she nodded. "Okay, I'll see you there." he said, and handed the operating list back to her. "Believe me Katrina, I've taken all the comments from Dr. Davidson to heart, and I'm not going to overload my lists. I've been good so far, haven't I? And I'm trying not to have to put too much on the emergency lists." He smiled at her, and she smiled back. "See you tonight" he muttered, and was gone.
Katrina sat at the desk, and pulled the work list towards her. She was allocating staff when Eleanor walked into the office. "Sorry, I misled you" she said. "I must have picked up the wrong list" she smirked at her sister, and glanced at the list that Katrina was working on. "Just want to see who is going to be scrubbing for Simon tomorrow" she said. "I'm learning so much from him already, and I'm looking

forward to scrubbing with him again tomorrow. He's got that big aneurysm on the list which he's going to let me assist him with. But I wondered, are you doing anything tonight?" Katrina shook her head. "No," she said, not wanting to let her sister know that she was going to go out with Simon. "But I don't fancy being sociable tonight. I might have a quiet evening, and get on with doing some more work on the Dame's costume. It's just a question of giving it some more embellishments at the moment. I'm tired after yesterday, I think. I'll see you tomorrow, if that's okay." Her sister nodded, left the office, and Katrina wondered what Eleanor would say if she found out that her sister was going to have a drink with her new boss.

That evening, she dressed carefully for her drink with Simon, eventually deciding on a light blue skirt and a white blouse, covered it with a deep blue coat, and walked to the pub, where she met up with him. He was dressed casually, instead of the suit he usually wore at work, and looked younger than he appeared at the hospital, and his smile, as she approached him, was friendly. "Hello" he said. "What would you like to drink?"

"Can I have a glass of white wine please" she said, and watched as he went to the bar to get her a drink. When he came back to the table he had been sitting at, with her drink, he handed it over, and they sat together. "Why did you invite me for a drink?" she asked, and he looked quizzically at her. "Because I want to get to know you a bit better" he said. "Why shouldn't I want to do that?"

"I thought we haven't getting on too well. After all, I've stopped you doing some operations in the past, and I thought you might have resented that."
"I don't resent it" he answered her, "I know you're just doing your job really, but I'll try and push it a bit if I can, to get the operations done. I don't mean to be difficult. I'm sorry if I've appeared that way in the past." He hesitated, then "Your face seemed very familiar to me, the first time we were introduced. Did I know you before I came here? Have we met before?"
"Yes, you were a junior reg. at St. Anselm's when I was a student nurse. We saw each other then, but you never acknowledged me."
"I can't think why not?" he said. "What were you like as a student nurse then?" and he grinned at her. She thought back to her time as a student nurse before she replied. "Harassed by sisters and staff nurses, running against time, trying to get everything done by a certain hour, and studying for exams. Believe me, I wouldn't have had any time if anybody had tried to strike up a friendship with me."
"When were you a student?" he asked, and she gave him the dates of her training. "I worked as a staff nurse on the medical wards for 12 months after I qualified, then managed to get a place on the theatre course here, and left. I got a job as a staff nurse after I'd completed the course, then got promoted and finally became senior sister about two years ago. What about you? You didn't stay at St. Anselm's all that time, did you?"
"No, I was there for about two years after I qualified, which is when we would have been there at the

same time, but I disappeared off to St. Davids to get more experience, I've moved around as you probably know, but I went to St. Jorus's as a junior consultant, then came to Queens when the job was advertised. I enjoy doing my job as you can probably realise, I like teaching the junior staff and getting their knowledge to a decent level. Mind you, some of them, well you wonder how they ever managed to pass their student exams. They come to the hospital, full of new ideas, but half of them don't have the faintest idea of how to operate, don't know one end of a scalpel from another, and I wouldn't let them loose on any of my patients." She grinned at his answers, for she knew exactly what he meant. "I don't know if you can remember any of the people, you were a student with, can you?"
"Some," he answered, "who do you mean?"
"Do you know David Howarth?" she asked, and Simon nodded. "Yes, Dave and I were good friends when we were at medical school." he paused, then "Hang on, the name is the same. Is he a relative?"
"Yes, David is my eldest brother. He's a medical consultant at White Bay Hospital, and is doing quite well. He asked me to say hello to you, the next time I saw you to talk to, but I must admit I forgot until just now."
"I lost touch with him when I left St. Anselm's. He was still there, but he decided to specialise in medicine. Could you give him my phone number and ask him to give me a bell, or give me his number, and I'll phone him."
"I'll give him your number. He often works quite long hours, so I don't know when he'll be able to

contact you."
"Good grief, who would have thought it?" Simon said, "I mean, you and I working together, when David and I were at med. School together. Is he your only brother?"
"No, I've got another one, James, who is a senior paramedic. He hated doing exams, so he went sideways, if you know what I mean, and started working on the ambulances, and now he's a controller, and I've got a sister, who's a doctor as well."
"Didn't you want to become a doctor?" he asked, but she shook her head, concealing the truth, and answering the way she had done, since she had started her training. "I like looking after people. I got all the exams I needed to go to medical school, but I decided to nurse instead. My father was a consultant orthopaedic surgeon, and mum was a nurse before they got married, so I didn't stand a chance of doing anything else really, did I?" She hesitated, then, "What about you, do you have any relatives who are in the profession?" He shook his head. "No, I've got two sisters, but they are both married and they've got children now."
He grinned, and changed the subject, and they sat drinking together and talking. They found out they shared the same interests in books and music, and when she said she liked classical music, he grinned. "So, you wouldn't object if I put classical music on the radio in theatre tomorrow?"
"I wouldn't object at all" she said, "but it all depends on the other staff. They might not like hearing Beethoven or Brahms, in the background."

"Well, tough" he said. "I'm the surgeon, so what I say, goes" They grinned together, and she began to feel relaxed in his presence. By the time, the landlord called time, they were laughing together enjoying each other's company. "I'll walk you home" he said, as they stood and put their coats on. "Would you like to come out again? Maybe we could have a meal somewhere?"

"I'd like that" Katrina said as he took her hand and escorted her from the pub. When they reached the block of flats where she lived, she stopped, and indicated that they had arrived. "I live on the first floor" she said. "Thanks for seeing me home."

"What are you doing this weekend?" he asked and she replied without hesitation, "Absolutely nothing. Why?"

"Just wondered if you fancied coming out for a meal then? I'm not on call, so we could meet up on Saturday and go and find a restaurant somewhere if that would suit you."

"Okay" she nodded. "That would be nice." He grinned at her. "I'll come and pick you up about 7.00 if that would be okay? Do you have any preference about types of food?"

"No" she answered, "I eat anything and everything."

"Okay. I'll see you tomorrow. Are you still going to scrub for me?" She nodded. "Yes, I've put myself and Anne on the list. She'll do the first case, and I'll scrub for the aneurysm." He smiled at her, and she felt something go through her body, a frisson of something, and knew that despite all she had said about him in the past, she did like him. "Sleep well" he said, bent his head and kissed her gently on her cheek. "Goodnight" she whispered, and she went into the building, watched by Simon, who had a smile on his face.

Chapter Three

When she woke the next morning, Katrina lay for a few minutes remembering the way she had laughed and joked with Simon the night before, and the way she had felt at the end of the evening. She sighed, decided that she would let life go on as it was, and got out of bed ready for work. The lists for that day were quite long, and she had already told one of the surgeons that he would have to cut them down, as they were likely to over-run, and she wouldn't have enough late staff on duty to be able to continue with them. As she went into the theatre to assist Anne with laying up for the first case, she smiled to herself, for the surgeons' attitudes had altered subtly in the last few weeks, since she had enlisted the help of Dr. Davidson. He made a point of coming to talk to her and asking if she had enough staff for the lists, and had told her that the committee were meeting very soon, and he should be able to give her good news about the number of staff who could be appointed. She put that to the back of her mind, and set about making sure that her staff were happy with their work for the day. Anne had laid up her trolley, the patient had arrived in the anaesthetic room, and everything was going well, when Eleanor arrived in theatres. "Oh Sister" she said, "I've just spoken to Mr. Parker, and he wants to re-order the list, and do the aneurysm first." she turned away, then, "See to it, will you."

"Impossible" said Katrina and Eleanor swung round to face her. "Why?" she asked. "Mr. Parker wants to do it first."

"If he'd told me that earlier, then I might have been able to prevent the anaesthetic nurse from sending for the patient, but as it is, the patient is here, is probably anaesthetised already, and I am not going to send him back to the ward, and have to bring him back again, after the aneurysm patient is operated on." She turned away. "You'll just have to let him know you didn't tell us in time." Eleanor gave her a dirty look. "You tell him" she said, and walked away. Anne and Katrina watched her go, and Anne said softly, "I told you we were going to have problems with that one. I'm all right here, go and find him and tell him, and I'll stand by to pick up the pieces." Katrina nodded, and walked out of the theatre and looked around for Simon. He was in the office, and had just put the phone down, when she walked in. "Hello" he said, with a smile, "Problems?" She shook her head. "No, not really," she replied, "but I've just been informed that you wanted to do the aneurysm first, but the Laparotomy patient is already asleep, so I couldn't change the order of the list. Sorry."

"I didn't want to re-order the list" he said slowly. "Who told you that I did?"

"Your SHO, Dr. Howard," she replied, and glanced at his face. "Why would she tell me that you wanted to do the aneurysm first?" she asked, and his mouth grew grim. "I don't know" he said, "but I'm having to think about a few things. Let the list go on as it is, and I'll think about the situation, and talk to you later." he smiled at her. "Did you sleep well?" he asked softly, and she nodded. "Yes thanks" she said, and smiled. "I'll go back and see if Anne is okay." and she walked out of the office and back into the laying up room. “Was he okay about it?” Anne asked and she nodded. “There's something going on, and I don't know what it is.” she said softly. “He didn't want the order of the list changed at all.” Anne looked surprised. “Why did Doctor Howard tell us that he did then?” she asked, but Katrina shook her head. “I don't know. I think he's going to talk to her and find out just what is going on. She gave me a list yesterday which had seven large cases on it, two aneurysms and five laparotomies, and when I queried it, she told me he was too busy to come and see me, and he...” she stopped, not willing to complete the sentence, “but he came, said he hadn't been busy, and gave me the revised list. When he looked at the list she’d given me, he said we'd already operated on them, including the appendix that turned out to be the aneurysm patient that I had to stay so late in order to operate on, and most of them were going home soon. When she came back, she said she must have picked up the wrong list, but she couldn't have done. She must have deliberately picked the names out of the operating book. She's definitely trying to cause a bit of a problem.” Just then, the anaesthetic room doors opened, and the patient was bought into theatre, and what with all the rush of making sure that the patient was in the correct position, she forgot about it. Simon came into the theatre, and assisted in the positioning, before sending his registrar and Eleanor to scrub, and when he was satisfied that everything was okay, he went to do the same. Katrina had made sure that the surgeons’ gowns and gloves were ready, and when they were tied into the gowns, she stood back, to allow them access to the patient, and provided a small stool for Eleanor to stand on, to be at the right height for the operation. Anne was ready and waiting for them, and with the patient draped, she took the bowl that the scalpel was in, and allowed Simon to take it, and the operation commenced. As usual, he worked fast, but Katrina was able to have a quick coffee break, before she went to get the sets ready for the next operation. When she got back into theatre, she could definitely sense a bit of an atmosphere, and wondered what had been said, but she sent the auxiliary for her coffee break, and stood waiting to give Anne any assistance she required. "Katrina, could I have some more swabs please?" Anne asked, and Katrina opened a package onto the trolley. The two girls counted them together, and Katrina carefully added the number to the board, ready for the final swab count. At the end of the operation, before Simon started to close the patient, Anne was doing the first count with Katrina, and they were one small swab short. "Swab count is not correct Mr. Parker" Anne announced, and he looked surprised. "Are you sure?" he asked and she nodded. "We'll do it again," Katrina said, and the count took place a second time. "Still incorrect Mr. Parker" Anne announced, and the surgeon shook his head, and started to investigate the wound to make sure that a swab had not been left inside. "Call X Ray please" Simon said, after the girls had made sure that the swab was not on the floor or on the trolley. By this time, a large amount of time had passed, and Katrina was turning to go to the phone, to call X Ray, and ask them to bring the portable machine to theatre to X

Ray the patient, and hopefully locate the missing swab, when out of the corner of her eye, she watched in amazement, as her sister surreptitiously produced the missing swab from where it had been pushed under one of the drapes, and pushed it onto the floor. "Hold it" she said now. "I think I've just seen it. Doctor Howard, why were you hiding that swab?" Eleanor looked up surprised, but Katrina knew that she had to make a stand. "I've just seen you pull it out from under the drape and drop it on the floor" she said now. "This can wait until after the patient is off the table, but you and I are going to have a chat afterwards" She turned to Anne. "Let's try that again." she said, and picking up the swab that Eleanor had dropped onto the floor, she hung it up, before she and Anne counted the swabs again. This time, the count was correct, and leaving Anne to be attended to by the auxiliary, she went to get scrubbed and lay up for the aneurysm. She was soon ready, and able to go back into theatre, to assist with getting the patient off the table. Simon was definitely not happy with the delay, and watched as his patient was taken into the recovery area. "Would you come with me please, Doctor Howard?" she said, and led the way to the office to confront her sister. When Eleanor entered the office, Katrina shut the door behind her, and turned to see the other girl smiling at her. "What the hell do you think you are playing at, Eleanor?" she asked angrily. "You've already lied to me once today about Mr. Parker wanting to change the order of the list, and now you've delayed the second patient, because you thought it would be fun to hide a swab! You can't do

these things Elly. You're not making yourself very popular, I can tell you. What on earth do you think you are doing?"
"Nothing" said Eleanor. "I just thought I'd keep you all on your toes. Hiding a swab seemed to be the ideal way of making sure that you all know what you are doing."
"Well, it's not funny, and you don't need to make sure we know what we are doing. We are all qualified nurses, qualified theatre nurses I might add, and we've been doing this job a lot longer than you have. We all know what to do, better than junior doctors" said Katrina, her anger dying down "I mean it Elly, if you do anything else like that, or try and change things that don't need to be changed, then something is going to be said, and I will do my best to get you transferred back to St. Anselm's. You're only on a scholarship at the moment, but I'm sure that something could be arranged to get another SHO allocated to the list. Do I make myself clear?"
Eleanor nodded. "I'm sorry Katy, really, I am. It just seemed to be a bit of fun."
"Well, it's not" Katrina said. "This department is busy enough without having to worry about sorting out your little tricks. Mr. Parker has been okay about it so far, but if it happens again, then believe me, he'll blow his top, and I'm sure you can remember what that was like when he blew up when we were at St. Anselm's." Eleanor nodded, for the occasion when Simon had lost his temper at his previous hospital, was still talked about by the staff who had been on duty then. "Right, so no more stupid pranks" she said. "I'm going to go and scrub again now, and if

you so much as breathe out of place, believe me, I shall ask that you be removed from theatre, and as I'm the senior nurse, my request will be allowed." Eleanor nodded and smiled at her sister. "Sorry Katy, honest I am. Don't ask for me to be excluded. I need to learn the way that Simon does these aneurysms, and this is a good one to learn on."
"Well, don't try anything then." Katrina opened the door and went out into the corridor, to walk along to the theatre, and opened the door. The patient was being positioned on the table, arms outstretched and tied loosely into place, and she knew she had time to re-scrub and get ready to assist the surgeon. "All okay Sister?" Simon asked, and she nodded. "I think so." she replied. "I'll get ready for the operation." and she went to re-scrub. Eleanor came back into theatre, along with the registrar, and Simon looked at her. "Have you had a drink?" he asked, and when she shook her head, he said "go and have a quick drink, then come back and assist us. This is going to be a long operation, and I don't want you passing out halfway through because you've not had anything to drink." Eleanor didn't say anything, just turned and went back to the coffee room, and Katrina gave a sigh of relief. Nothing else was said, and the operation got underway. Eleanor came back into the theatre and scrubbed up, and went to stand by Simon. By the time they came to the end of the surgery, Katrina felt drained. She'd been on edge all the time she'd been scrubbed, waiting for Eleanor to do something, and now they had got to the end of the operation, all she wanted to do was sit down, and relax. She was hungry as well, and when the

patient had been taken to the intensive care unit, she ensured that Anne was okay to scrub for the final operation, and went into the coffee room, to make a drink, and eat her sandwiches. The rest of the day passed without incident, the surgeons thanked her at the end of the lists, and as she made her way home that evening, she was deep in thought about what she should do. Eventually, she decided to do nothing at the moment, but knew that if anything else happened, she was going to have to talk to David. She knew that Eleanor was on call that evening, along with Simon, so she wouldn't have anybody to talk to about the day's events, and as she opened the door of the flat, she knew that she was lonely. Wearily, she cooked herself a small meal, drank the tea she had made and had just sat down afterwards, when the phone rang. It was her mother, ringing from the boat, to tell her when she would be home, and when she put the phone down, she felt a lot happier. Her mother and father had always wanted to go on a long cruise, and when her father retired, they had been able to fulfil that ambition. She had promised to go and see them in a couple of weeks' time, and knew that she had missed them. She smiled to herself, then remembered her promise to Simon the night before. He had written his phone number on a page of her diary, and she needed to let David have it, so phoned him. Her talk with her older brother was good. He was glad to receive Simon's phone number and promised to talk to him soon, but when he asked how Eleanor was getting on, Katrina hesitated. "What's she done?" David asked, and Katrina, going against all her good intentions, told him what had been happening. “I didn't think it would be a good idea for you two to be in the same theatre.” he said now. “I know you, and I remember how she can behave when she wants something, or somebody. I hope she's not trying to get her claws into Simon. Unless he's changed a lot, he might be susceptible.”

“Don't the rest of the girls in my theatre stand a chance then?” she asked. “The way you are talking makes it sound as though she's the only one he would try and date.”

“I didn't mean it like that” David laughed at her. “Has he ever shown any interest in anybody else in theatre, or in the hospital?”

“Not that I've heard of” she admitted, not wanting to tell him that she was going out to dinner with him on Saturday. David hesitated, then continued “Elly's different to a lot of you girls. She wants to marry a wealthy man, and I know that Simon doesn't only rely on his salary, he's got another income, or so he once told me. Once she's decided upon a man, she'll do her utmost to get him. She's decided that being a doctor is a good stepping stone. She's insidious, she'll try to creep in, get him interested and finally he'll end up married to her, and he won't know how it happened. Just remember what happened with you and John. I know you are twins, Katy, but you've got a completely different attitude to life. You always defer to her, and let her have her own way. Well, what happens when you both decide you want the same man? You let her have John, didn't you? Are you always going to let her have your man, even if you want him for yourself?”

"Well, I can't imagine anybody wanting me" Katrina said, "so the question doesn't arise, does it?" She laughed. "I'll sit back and watch her technique, then I can learn from it."
"Well take care Katy, I wouldn't want you hurt by your own twin sister."
"After the rocket I gave her in the office this morning, I don't think she'll try much more in theatre" Katrina said, and David gave a short laugh. "I wouldn't bet on that, Katy. But phone me if you need somebody to have a talk with her, and I'll try and help. Anyway, I've got work to be getting on with, so I'll say goodnight, and speak to you soon. Take care Katy."
They said their farewells, and she hung up, wondering if what David had said about Eleanor wanting Simon was true. She smiled to herself, Simon had asked her out, hadn't asked her sister, and she was looking forward to Saturday evening. She made herself another drink, and went to bed with her book, to sleep soundly all night.

As Simon only had operating lists on two days a week, she did not expect to see him again until Saturday evening, but it was as she was doing the ordering in the office on Thursday afternoon, that he came in to see her. "So, what happened when you had Eleanor in here yesterday?" he wanted to know, but she shook her head. "I told her that I wasn't happy with the way she had behaved that day, and told her that if she carried on as she was doing, deliberately hiding swabs, and lying to me about you wanting to change the order of the list, then I would do my best to get her removed and sent back to St. Anselm's. I told her that behaviour like that would not be tolerated. She apologised, and promised not to do anything like that again."

"You were very tense during the operation" he said. "Were you watching to make sure she didn't do anything like that again?" Katrina nodded. "Once somebody has done that once, it makes everybody a bit worried that they will do it again. This is my theatre unit, and I don't want it to be an unhappy unit, and it will be, if something like that happens again."

"Do you want me to have a chat with her about it?" he asked, but she shook her head. "No, not at the moment, thanks. I hope that what I said will cause her to have a re-think about the way she's acting, but if it happens again, then I might have to get you involved." He smiled at her. "Okay, you're the boss. I've got to go, but I'll see you on Saturday evening." and with another smile, he was gone.

Later that afternoon, Eleanor came into the office to talk to her. "Am I forgiven?" she asked with a smile, but Katrina knew she had to be firm with her sister. "As long as you don't do anything like that again" she said. "You could have caused real problems you know, and people won't want to work with you if you do anything like that again."

"I know," Eleanor sighed. "I'm really sorry Katy. I knew it was wrong, but I didn't think it through properly" she smiled at her sister. "Please Katy forgive me. Tell you what, I'm off this weekend, why don't we go out on Saturday night and have a meal

and go dancing? I'll pay for us both just to say I'm sorry." Katrina was about to accept, when she remembered. "Sorry Elly," she said, "I'm already booked for Saturday evening."
"Who's taking you out then?" her sister asked, but Katrina didn't want to tell her sister the truth. "Oh, I'm just going out with some of the pantomime people" she said. "We try and get together as often as we can, and this Saturday has been arranged for a long time."
"Okay" Eleanor said. "As it happens, one of the other SHO's did ask me out, so I'll go with him and we can probably go out together some other time. Would that be okay by you?" Katrina nodded. "I'll let you know my off duty when I've done it, and we can get together. Did you hear that mum and dad are coming back next week?" she changed the subject hurriedly, not wanting to tell her sister her plans. "I've said I'll try and get to see them in a week or two. Dave said he'll try and get to see them when he can as well."
"Have you been talking to David?" Eleanor asked slowly, and Katrina nodded. "I had to give him a phone number. He'd asked me if I could find it for him, so I phoned him to let him know."
"Whose phone number did he want" Eleanor asked, and unwilling to tell her the truth, Katrina prevaricated. "One of David's friends had been trying to get in contact with the pantomime group here, but had lost the phone number of the guy who organises it, so I was able to give it to him." That part was true, but that conversation had taken place a few weeks earlier, but the explanation satisfied

Eleanor, who looked at her watch as she got up. "Gotta go" she said. "I'll see you next week. Okay?" Katrina nodded, and watched as her sister left the office. Things were getting complicated, she thought to herself.

When Saturday evening arrived, Katrina was ready and waiting when Simon came to pick her up. She was wearing a long sleeved, burgundy coloured dress, which suited her colouring. Her hair was caught back in a clip, and hanging loosely around her shoulders, and she looked very pretty. As she opened the door to Simon, she saw his eyes light up as he saw her, and knew that he appreciated the way she looked. He was wearing a grey suit, with a white shirt and a dark silk tie, and looked extremely smart. "I thought it might be a good to go a bit further out of town" he said, after he had greeted her. "There are some good restaurants around here, but some of the better ones are a bit further out, so we've got a bit of a drive to get to the one I think you might like." She nodded, caught up her bag and was ready to go. He saw her eyes light up as she saw his car – a Bentley, and grinned as he shut his door and did up his seat belt. "I like driving, but I needed something that would be comfortable on long journeys, and this fits the bill."
"It's lovely" she said. "There's so much room in it. My Mini will seem very small after this." The talk turned to cars and she didn't realise how far they were going. "So, whereabouts is this restaurant?" she asked, and was surprised when he said quietly, "Near Reading."

"But that's miles away" she said, "not that I'm not enjoying the drive, because I am, but it's a long way away just for a meal."
"It's a good restaurant" he answered slowly, "and also its far enough away, that we're very unlikely to see anybody from the hospital there. I'm not being selfish; I just don't want our first date to be spoilt by acquaintances from the hospital coming up and making small talk. Do you object to that?" She shook her head, for she had been slightly worried about that possibility herself. "No." she said quietly. "Thank you for thinking about it." The drive continued, and soon they were entering the forecourt of the restaurant. He opened her door for her and escorted her inside. The restaurant was quiet, there were plenty of people there, but the chatter was subdued, and she knew that it was going to be expensive, and wondered if her dress were suitable. Obviously, it was, for they were escorted to a table, given a menu to peruse and their order for drinks taken. Katrina had opted for a glass of wine, but David had chosen a low alcohol lager, and she grinned at his choice. "What are you smirking at?" he asked lightly, and she shook her head. "Sorry, it just seems unfair that you should have to have something like that, because you're driving."
"Well, next time you can drive" he said, "or invite me to your flat and cook me a meal, then I can have something to drink."
"Okay" Katrina said without thinking. "What would you like me to cook for you?" then she opened her eyes wide, as she realised what she had said, and Simon laughed at her. "We'll talk about that later on,

shall we?" he asked, and looked at the menu. They had made their choice, given the order to the waiter, and were talking about work. "So why did Eleanor change her name?" he asked, and without thinking, Katrina answered, "because she didn't want to get confused with David, when they were working at the same hospital" then realised what he had said, and stared at him. "How did you know?" she asked, and he grinned at her. "I don't think you realise how much you resemble each other" he said. "When you've got a mask on, your eyes are exactly the same, and if you'd changed places at the table, I don't know if anybody would have worked out that you had."

"Oh, come off it," she said, "I'm a couple of inches taller than she is, and probably a dress size bigger than her as well."

"Also," he continued as if she hadn't spoken, "David told me that his sisters were working together, and he didn't think it was a very good idea." They laughed together, at his comment, but then Katrina's laughter faded. "No, and he was right" Katrina said. "We normally get on well together when we're not working, but since she arrived, I've felt tense all the time, and I know she's trying to upset me, and show me up. I don't know why she's doing it – after all, she's a doctor, and as she takes great delight in telling me, I'm only a nurse."

"You are not 'only' a nurse" he said angrily, his hand coming to cover hers as it lay on the table. "You're a damn good theatre Sister, you run that place very well, everybody likes you, and you don't want to let her hurt you. Dave and I had quite a conversation

about the pair of you, when he phoned. What's she done to you in the past to give you such an inferiority complex?" Katrina wondered what else her brother had said about the pair of them, for he had known things that had happened when they were still living at home. "Oh, little things" she said, liking the feel of his hand on hers, "she started it, when we were at school, we were more alike then, she'd tell the teachers that I'd done something, when it was her, and it got worse as we got older. Until I grew taller than she was, people couldn't tell us apart, and I put on weight on my face, and we became much less identical. When we went to our senior school, we were placed in different classes, and she had her own group of friends, as did I, but she was always the ring leader of her group, and I was just one of the girls. I know mum got a bit worried about things, but there was nothing she could do about it, and I just got on with things, got my head down and studied hard, but Elly just sailed through the exams, didn't seem to need to study at all, and got really upset when I did better than she did. I got higher grades than she did in our O Levels, but when we did our A levels, she decided she'd have to work harder, and we got identical grades. She'd always wanted to be a doctor, and so had I, but somehow her application for medical school went ahead, and mine didn't. None of us knew what happened, and by the time they'd investigated everything, it was too late to go ahead. So, she started at medical school, Mum, Dad and I had a long chat, and between us we decided that I should apply to be a nurse instead."
"What happened with the medical school?" he

asked. "Surely they must have received your application?"
"No" she said quietly. "That was the problem. Somehow my application managed to get lost in the post, which is what the medical school said, but it was odd that of two applications, posted together, one should manage to get lost. Especially as they were both sent registered mail as we were advised to do, as all our certificates were included. And I'd put my address on the back of the envelope as well, so it should have been able to be returned, but it never turned up. By the time we'd managed to get duplicates, it was too late." His hand tightened on hers, and at that moment, the waiter bought their first course, and they started to eat. They didn't talk any more about her problems with Eleanor, instead talked about anything and everything, and Katrina found herself able to tell him things she hadn't been able to say for a long time. At the end of the meal, as they sat drinking coffee, he bought the subject back to Eleanor's arrival in the theatres. "What else has she done to you?" he asked. "I know there's something, but I think you buried it a long time ago. David said he was worried about you, but he didn't tell me everything. I hope you can tell me about it."
Katrina drew in a deep breath, then started to speak. "It happened when we were nearly 24, and I was working as a senior staff nurse in theatres. She was in her final year at med. School, and had been sent to work at the Queens country unit, so we were quite close to each other, and we saw a lot of each other. She was doing very well. I met somebody – a doctor, John, who was an anaesthetist, and we got very

friendly, went out together, and finally he asked me to marry him. I didn't feel sure about it, didn't know if he was the only man for me, I wanted time to think about it, and foolishly I told Eleanor about him. She said she was pleased for me, and we all got together for a meal. She acted nice at first, then gradually things started to go wrong. They would meet up for a drink, when I was working, or if we were together, she started to very carefully denigrate me, told him things about me, things that I'd forgotten, that made him laugh, and got him interested in her, and somehow after that, our friendship started to lessen. He fell for her big time, and she led him on. Finally, he very sheepishly told me he no longer wanted to marry me, but hoped I'd be happy with him as my brother-in-law instead, because he wanted to marry Elly. I was hurt, even though I'd already decided I didn't want to marry him, but I accepted it. They got as far as setting the date, and asking me to be bridesmaid, and then she dropped him like a stone, handed him back his ring, and left Mum and I to try and sort out the situation. She hurt him badly, thought it was extremely funny, but nobody else did. He moved away, and he's now working up North. We're still friends, but I can't forgive her for what she did to either of us. I don't tell her if I've been invited out for a date, because I know she'd try and spoil it for me. I haven't mentioned that you invited me out, so please don't tell her." she suddenly realised that he was Eleanor's boss, and then knew she had to apologise for what she had said. "I'm sorry Simon, I shouldn't be telling you all my problems, should I?"
"Katrina, I'm hardly likely to tell the junior doctor on

my team who I'm taking out, am I? Don't worry, I won't say a thing. But I hope it's not going to stop me taking you out again? I was joking when I said you could cook for me, but I'd like to take you out again soon."

"I don't mind cooking for you" she said, aware that she did like him, and felt that he liked her. "I've always enjoyed cooking, and I love trying new recipes."

"Okay" he said, "when are you off again?" She gave him her off duty details, and before they left the restaurant, they had arranged another date for later on that week. It was late when he looked at his watch, and reluctantly suggested that they should be going. He helped her on with her coat, and they went out to the car together. The night was cold, and she shivered, and he put his arm around her shoulders, and drew her close to him. The drive home was pleasant, and she knew she had enjoyed the evening, very much. As they got out of the car, when they arrived at her flat, he smiled at her. "Do you mind if I call you Katy?" he asked. "Dave always calls you that, but I've never heard anybody else do it."

"I don't mind" she said, "but please not when we're working together. I'd prefer to be Katrina in theatres. I've always been called that when I'm working." He grinned as he said, "no it wouldn't be very professional, would it? But Katy it shall be when we're outside work." and he bent his head to kiss her on her cheek. "Do you want to come up for coffee?" she asked, and he nodded, and they walked up the stairs to the flat. She opened the door, and they went into the sitting room, but when she would have gone to the kitchen, he stopped her, bent his head, and kissed her. When he drew back, she stared up at him, and he smiled again, before he bent his head. The kiss lasted a long time, and his arms were holding her close to him. "That's better than coffee, isn't it?" he muttered, before kissing her again. She felt at home in his arms, and felt lost when he drew back. "Perhaps I won't stay for coffee after all." he said softly. "I'd better go, and let you get some sleep. I'm rushing things." he kissed her gently again, and looked down at her. "I'll see you at work on Monday" he said quietly. "Sleep well Katy. Goodnight" then he was gone, the door closing quietly behind him. Katrina prepared for bed in a thoughtful mood. He had made her feel very wanted, and she wanted to keep her memories to herself for a while. She knew she would say nothing to Eleanor, when they saw each other again, and as she turned the lights out, smiled to herself at the secret she was keeping.

Chapter Four

Simon's list for Wednesday was very involved and Katrina had to spend quite a long time on Tuesday, trying to make sure that all the instruments needed for the operation were available. She hadn't scrubbed for him on Monday, knowing that she had to separate her work life and her personal life, and although she wanted to see him again, she had decided to stay away. He had greeted her politely that morning, and she had been polite to him in return when they had cause to speak to each other. She did her work in her usual fashion, buoyed up by the fact that he had asked her to go out with him again on Thursday evening, and she was looking forward to it. Eleanor had visited her on Monday evening, as she was not on call, full of details of what she had done, and who she had been with on Saturday evening, and trying to pin Katrina down for a date when the two girls could go out together, but there didn't seem to be an opportunity in the next couple of weeks. Katrina was going home to see her parents the following weekend, and Eleanor would be on call, so the two girls agreed to get together after that if it were possible. "Did I hear right, that you made a dress for Keith Jenkins?" she asked and Katrina had nodded. "Let me see it then, please" Eleanor begged and Katrina had shown her the complete costume. Her sister had laughed heartily, at the thought of the senior orthopaedic surgeon fitting into it, and for a time, Katrina had hoped that they were going to be able to continue the relationship they had enjoyed before Eleanor came to work at the same hospital, but she didn't somehow think they would be able to. “I've got to take it to rehearsal next week, and hand it over to him” she said. “I was meant to be going tonight, but I was too tired to go out. Of course,” she continued, with a grin “I could always take it into work and give it to him, but I don't want to spoil the surprise for people who go and see the hospital pantomime.” Eleanor agreed, and soon left her sister to have an early night. The list that day had not been too bad, had only over run, by about five minutes, but Katrina felt tired, and hadn't really wanted her sister to visit, but she couldn't say so. The following days lists were better, with no problems, and Katrina felt better after a long sleep, and had just sat down to have a quiet cup of tea on her own, when the bell rang, and inwardly cursing whoever it was at the door, she went to open it. Simon was standing on the doorstep, and her face lit up with a smile. “Hello” he said, as she allowed him entry. “I didn't want to wait until Thursday, so I thought I'd come and see you tonight. Is that okay?” he asked anxiously, and she nodded. He put his arms around her, held her tight, and kissed her hard. The kiss lasted a long time, and when he raised his head, she was breathless. “Shall I make you some coffee?” she asked with a smile, and he laughed, as he remembered what had happened on Saturday night. “Yes, please” he replied. “And this time, perhaps I'll actually have a cup.” She laughed at him, told him to have a seat, and went to the kitchen. She was putting coffee into the cups, when he came up behind her, put his arms around her, held her close to him and kissed her neck.

"That's better" he said, as she turned round, and bent his head to kiss her again. "Simon, if you want coffee, you'll have to let me make it" she said, and unwillingly, he released her, watched as she poured hot water onto the granules, added milk, and handed him the mug. "Now, come and sit down, for heaven's sake" she urged him into the sitting room, and they sat down on the settee, placing their mugs on the coffee table in front of them. "That's even better" he said, as she sat beside him, and he put an arm around her, and drew her close to him. His lips were demanding on hers, and she gave herself up to the moment, knowing that she was enjoying their closeness. "I wonder what David would say if he could see what I'm doing at the moment?" he said when he lifted his lips away from hers, and she smiled. "Well, I don't know whether he would want his friends to get involved with us." Simon grinned, "Oh I'm more than involved" he said, as he kissed her again. "Actually," Katrina said softly, "my other brother, James would like both of us to have relationships, but David never says anything about us having one. I can't remember when he last had a girlfriend. When I last saw him, he said there was nobody special. Certainly, he's not had a girlfriend for a couple of years, that he's introduced to the rest of the family."

"Don't say anything, will you but I was thinking that perhaps men would be more in his line" Simon said quietly, and Katrina gasped. "I don't think I've thought about it as deeply as you obviously have" she said. "But it would explain a few things. Oh, poor David. I hope he'll be able to get together with somebody at some stage." Simon took her hand in his. "Don't whatever you do, talk to him about it. I think I noticed it first, when we were at medical school, we had a couple of loners like him in the group, and they turned out to be happier with members of their own sex. But I haven't seen him for quite a while, so I don't know if I'm correct. If I'm right, and its only my thought, then he might take a time before he finds his one and only. But you never know" he laughed, "he might have found somebody already. As you don't see him very often, you probably wouldn't know, would you? Would your parents be okay with it, if I'm right?" Katrina thought for a moment, then nodded. "They're very liberal minded. I don't think they'd object. They'd only want him to be happy. And if having a male partner would make him happy, they would be happy." Simon kissed her cheek. "I'm sorry, I didn't mean to upset you" he said, but she smiled at him. "I'm not upset." she replied. "I just didn't have a clue. Shows how unobservant I am about those types of things."

"Well, you've got a lot of other things on your mind." he said, "such as, how long these accursed surgeons are going to take over their cases, and will you be able to get off duty at a decent hour, and are you going to be able to get some more staff?"

"And what's the answer to those questions?" Katrina asked, and grinned as he replied seriously, "well, the first case tomorrow is going to be the big one. It will go over lunch, and might even over-run at the end. If nobody else runs over, then you should be able to get off duty on time, and as to more staff, I haven't heard anything from the committee. They met this

week, so you should be hearing from Ian Davidson very soon." He released her hand and picked up his coffee mug. "Are you going to be my scrub nurse tomorrow for my major case? It's going to be difficult, and I don't think anybody else has got the experience that you have."
"Oh" Katrina took a sip of coffee, then put it down on the coffee table and leant back against the back of the settee, "now I know why you've come to see me. It's just so you can ask me to scrub for you tomorrow, and do a case that's probably going to last hours and hours. Typical men!" She hid a smile, as Simon put his cup down, placing it on the coffee table beside hers. "It's not like that" he said earnestly. "I know I said I'd come and see you on Thursday, but when I got home tonight, I wasn't on call, I knew you were off duty tonight, and I very much wanted to do this" and he pulled her towards him, and kissed her long and hard. When he lifted his head, she was smiling, and he knew she'd been teasing him. "Tease" he growled, before kissing her again. Their positions had altered, and she was lying against him, almost on top of him, and when he broke the kiss, she smiled down at him. "Simon, I wanted you to come and see me this evening as well." she whispered. "I've thought about little else since Saturday night. Elly came to see me last night, and wondered why I was so tired, and I couldn't tell her that I'd been awake for a long time that night, thinking about what happened before you left." He rolled over, so she was under him, and his lips met hers again. "I did wonder" he said softly. "You looked tired yesterday, and I wondered if that had

been the reason. I'm sorry Katy." He kissed her again, then sat up, handed her the coffee mug, and took his from the table. Katrina took a drink, and smiled at him. "Yes," she answered his original question, "I am going to scrub for you tomorrow. I've already done the work list, and put myself and Janet on to your list."

"Thank you" he muttered. "Do you want me to tell you anything about it, or are you okay? I can tell you what I expect to do, if you want me to tell you."

"No," she was definite. "I know what you will probably want, so I'll be able to get on with the case. And you've only got one small case after that, so Janet will scrub for that."

"Barring any emergencies" he added and she nodded. "Provided we don't have any major staff sickness, things should go well tomorrow." and watched in amazement as he leant forward and touched the coffee table. "Have to touch wood when you say that" he said. "It's when you say things like that, that the emergencies come pouring in."

"I take it you don't want to put the minor case on first?" she asked, and he shook his head. "No, if the big one runs over time, then we can cancel it, or put it on the emergency list. Don't let anybody tell you otherwise."

"Okay boss" she said cheekily, and he grinned, as he kissed her again. "At least you know who your elders and your betters are" he said, and watched laughingly, as she shook her head. "Remember, they're my theatres, and if I don't want to scrub for you, then all I have to do is alter the work list so I'll

be doing a shorter and easier list." she warned him, and laughed as he looked penitently at her. "So, we've discussed work, and that's the end of it." he said. "Where do you want to go on Thursday? Do you want to stay local, or go further afield?"
"I don't mind at all." she replied. "You choose. If you want, you could come here and I'll cook something." He thought for a minute, then shook his head. "I'll take you out. You might be tired, and I don't want to overwork you, having to cook, when you come off duty."
"Well, I do normally cook something for myself" she answered him, "but going out for a meal sounds good." Simon nodded, "I'll think of somewhere to go." he said, then "Have you had any more trouble with Eleanor?" Katrina shook her head, "No, she's been remarkably well behaved yesterday and today. She came in, bought the list in, asked if I'd managed to arrange an ITU bed, and get the instruments and implants you wanted, and generally gave the impression of a well behaved SHO. She went out on Saturday evening, with one of the medical house officers, and came to see me last night, to tell me what I'd missed. I didn't tell her I hadn't missed anything, but we can't arrange to go out for a weekend together at the moment. I'm going home at the weekend to see my parents, as they've just come home from their cruise, and she's on call then, so we'll arrange something when she finds out her call rota." She took another sip of coffee and asked "You're on call this weekend, aren't you?" He nodded. "Yes, I swapped with Ewan a couple of weeks ago, because he wanted this weekend, and I

wasn't doing anything, so it was convenient. Where do your parents live? And when will you be back after visiting them?"
"Mum and Dad live near David, near White Bay Hospital, so it's only about 10 miles from here, but as they've been away on this cruise for the last ten weeks, I've said I'll go and stay with them, and we can catch up on all the news. I'll be able to leave early on Sunday evening, and get back here before 8.00 pm."
"So, if I were able to visit you on Sunday evening, would it be unwelcome?" he asked, and she shook her head. "No, of course not. You know you're welcome any time." At that, he leant forward, kissed her again, and they ended up laying side by side on the settee, their lips and hands touching. "That's very nice to know" he murmured as he lifted his head, his hands stroking her hair away from her face, before he kissed her again. "Oh Katy, I think I'm going too fast for you. Maybe I ought to go and let you get an early night, before tomorrow's operation."
"No, don't go. You're not going too fast" she said, as her hands touched his back. She had pushed his shirt away, and was touching his skin, and she could feel his heart rate increase as she did so. He was kissing her again, his hands holding her body close to his, and she could feel that he wanted her. She suddenly felt as she had when she had been with John, but knew that the feeling was deeper, more intense, and knew too, that she was in danger of falling in love with him. "I want you, but I'm not going to do anything tonight" he muttered against her lips,

before he kissed her again, his tongue exploring the sweetness within, and she smiled. He lifted his head, and looked down at her. "Why are you smiling?" he asked, but she shook her head, held his head between her hands, and kissed him. There was silence in the room for a long while, as they pleasured each other, with hands and mouth. At last, he lifted his head, and looked down at her, as she lay in front of him. He had undone the buttons on her blouse, and his fingers had moved the cup of the bra away, so that her nipples were exposed. "You look thoroughly debauched" he whispered, then bent and kissed her nipples. She gasped as sensations spread through her body, and she acknowledged that he was good at what he was doing. He had obviously had experience, she thought, and her mouth curved in a smile, as she realised, she was glad that he had. "How the hell am I going to face you across the operating table tomorrow, and not remember tonight?" he asked, and slowly and carefully rearranged her bra, so that her breasts were covered. "Well, it's going to be as bad for me, as it is for you" she replied. "Just remembering the feel of your hands on my body, and the way they make me feel" she sighed, "you'll have to forgive me if I go off into a brown study during the op."

"I won't give you the opportunity" he muttered. "And now, I really do think I ought to be going, so you can go to bed, and get some sleep." and he pushed himself upright. She lay where she was, and with a groan, he bent again, and kissed her. She didn't want him to go, wanted him to stay and make her whole, but knew that when he did take her, she wanted it to be when there was no opportunity of being disturbed, and they were both ready. He lifted himself off her body, and stood up. “Well, for a fleeting visit, which is what I thought this was going to be, it’s been very enjoyable” he said, tucking his shirt back into his trousers, as he did so. “Katy, I've got to go.” he said, and she drew her blouse around her. “I'll see you tomorrow, and then we can go for a meal on Thursday” He kissed her gently, then pulled her towards him, and gave her a hug. “Sleep well” he murmured, as his mouth met hers again, and she felt lost when he pulled away from her. “Goodnight little Katy” he muttered, and without a backward glance, he was gone. She stood where she was, thinking of the past hour, before she collected the mugs they had used, and put them in the sink to wash up. She prepared for bed, in something of a daze, and eventually turned out all the lights, and went to her bed, to lie and remember everything that had happened, as she drifted into a deep sleep.

The following morning, she was in the theatre, when he arrived in the department with Eleanor and Roger, his registrar. “Morning everybody” she heard him say, as they walked past, and she looked up, before giving her full attention to the trolley she was laying up. “This operation is going to be horribly complicated isn't it, Katrina?” Janet said, and she nodded in reply before Janet continued “It doesn't sound a very good one. I pity the poor patient. Being bought down to the anaesthetic room at 7.00 am, doesn't help, especially when he knows that the day staff don't come on duty until 8.00 am. I saw the ward nurse on her way back to the ward, and she said he's been so nervous, he didn't sleep at all last night, poor man."

"I think I'd be nervous too, if I had to have the same operation," Katrina said "This operation is going to be his best chance of a decent life, so hopefully everything will go well, and we'll be able to help him."

"It's a massive operation." Janet replied. "I've been told Mr. Parker is one of only four surgeons in the country to do it, and if we learn how to scrub for it, then if one of us goes for another job, we can say, yes, we can scrub for that, and hopefully that knowledge would assist us."

"Are you thinking about going for another job then?" Katrina hoped to goodness that the girl was going to say no, but her fears were realised. "My husband's job means that he might be moved around, so if he has to move, I'll have to find another job. If I can watch you scrubbing for this one, then I'll have a bit better idea, if he does another operation like this."

"Well, make sure you watch closely, what Sister does," Simon's voice made Katrina blush, as she recalled the night before, and she lifted her eyes to see Simon watching her. He was wearing a mask, but she saw his eyes crinkle at the corner, and knew he was smiling at her. "Good morning, Sister" he said now. "All prepared for today's little operation?"

"Yes Mr. Parker" she replied, "we sent for the patient at 7.00 am, and the anaesthetist started early, so we should be able to start soon."

"Good to hear" he said. "This operation is going to take a long time, so the earlier we can start, the

sooner we'll finish." he looked at her. "Do we have all the implants available to us?"
"Yes," she said, "They're all ready." She looked down at the trolley, unwilling to look directly at Simon "Have you had a good breakfast?" he asked and she raised her eyes to his. "Yes, thanks." she replied, "and I've got some sandwiches with me, if we do break for lunch. Don't worry about me. I'm accustomed to long operations."
"You might be" he said, "but you've not had to scrub for an all-day case like this one for a long time. I'll try and give us break mid-way through, but I don't know when it's going to be. I hope you're fit enough."
"Don't worry about me," she repeated. "I'm going to be fine. I hope your junior staff are going to be okay."
"They were warned about the length of the operation" he said, "so if they're not, they've only got themselves to blame." he grinned at her, and she saw the laughter light up his eyes. "I'll go and see how the anaesthetist is getting on" and he winked at her, as he walked away into the anaesthetic room.

That evening, as she walked slowly home, she reflected on the day. The operation had taken all day, and apart from a short break in the middle, when she had eaten her sandwich, she had been scrubbed for all of it. Eleanor hadn't been assisting all the time, having been called away in the middle to see a patient who had been admitted, but Simon and his registrar had been present for the entire operation. Luckily, she had some good staff, who had taken it on themselves to make sure that everything had been ordered, the work list for the next day had been done, and made sure that none of the other surgeons were experiencing any problems, so she could concentrate on the operation she was scrubbed for. At the end of the operation, Simon had thanked her for staying, and she had gone to have a cup of coffee, to try and relax before she went home. She hadn't been too impressed, therefore, when Eleanor had come into the coffee room and asked her if they could do the second case, straight afterwards. "No, Doctor Howard, it can't be done now." Katrina had explained, "we don't have enough staff to run three theatres. We've just finished an all-day case which has run late, Mr. Muir's list is carrying on, until he finishes the case, and the emergency list is taking place in theatre one. If Mr. Parker wants it to go on the emergency list, then we'll put it on, but it can't be done now."

"Oh, come on Sister" her sister had adopted the wheedling tone, she used when they were children together. "I'm sure you could find some staff to get it done now. I'm sure you'd be able to stay and do the case, if necessary."

"I said no, and I mean it." Katrina had been firm. "And as Mr. Parker has been scrubbed all day, I can't imagine he'd want to start again to get the case done." She took a sip of coffee, and smiled at her sister. "In any case," she added, "Mr. Parker asked me to arrange for the patient to be cancelled, while you were away from the table. The patient will go onto another list."

Eleanor looked askance at her sister. It wasn't very

often that Katrina got the better of her, and she wondered what she could do to make her sister look small. Suddenly she smiled, and Katrina wondered what was going on in her sister's head. "Sorry Sister" she said now. "Just teasing, honest."

"It didn't sound like teasing" came a voice from the doorway, and Eleanor jumped as she turned to see Simon standing in the doorway. "Don't push it, Doctor Howard. I know I've had enough for one day, and I'm sure that Sister Howarth has as well. Are you going home now Sister?" Katrina nodded, and he smiled at her. "Thanks again for the assistance" he said. "See you next week?" she smiled back at him, nodded and got up to go and get changed. "Goodnight, everybody" she said and went into the changing room. She hadn't seen her sister again, and as she unlocked the front door, she was glad to get home, to be able to relax. She had cooked herself a small meal, had a long relaxing bath and washed her hair, and was thinking about going to bed, when the phone rang. It was David, asking her if she would be visiting their parents that weekend, saying he would be there as well, and she was glad that he would be, for they were very good friends as well as being siblings, and she often felt closer to him, than she did to Eleanor. "I want to have a talk with you" he said, and she suddenly felt worried, for his tone was not as light as it had been. "Don't worry Katy, I'll explain when I see you. What are you doing the rest of the week?"

"I'm going out to dinner tomorrow night" she said, and grinned when he asked her who with.

"A friend" she replied, not wanting to tell him the

truth, and was surprised at his laugh. “Okay, you're not going to tell me, are you?” he said and she agreed with him. “I'm on my way to bed” she said now, “I've been scrubbed all day, so I've had a bath and I'm going to go to bed with a book, and get some sleep.”

“Okay, I won't keep you. Sleep well Katy. I'll see you at the weekend.”

As she disconnected, she wondered what he wanted to talk to her about, but decided she couldn't worry about it, before she talked to him, so turning off the lights, she went to bed.

The following day, she wasn't down to scrub for a list, so she was in the office, trying to make sense of the off duty, when Ian Davidson came to see her. He was accompanied by Miss Betts, and they were both wearing serious expressions. She offered them coffee, which was refused, and they made themselves comfortable in the office. “I have to give you some bad news” Ian Davidson said, and Katrina's heart sank. “The committee met this week, and they've decided that there isn't any money to be able to let you have more staff in the department. If anybody leaves, then that position won't be filled. I'm really sorry Katrina, I did my best for you. In addition, they have reiterated the fact that overtime won't be paid, and you must arrange for the time to be taken back in lieu, if you have to work overtime.”

“And how am I to manage to cover the operating lists without any staff? We're down seven people as it is.” she said. “I'm not the only theatre sister to want to know how she's meant to cover all these cases without any staff. The other theatres are in similar circumstances to me, and this department. We are going to be losing at least one staff nurse in the not-too-distant future, and we are now below the maximum number of staff required to cover the lists in any case. If anybody goes on holiday, or off sick, we are going to be in deep trouble."

"They say that there isn't a problem" she was told, and she looked at Miss Betts in disbelief. "How can they be so stupid?" she said angrily, "When was the last time they worked in an operating theatre?" she asked. "And why haven't they got the common courtesy to come and tell me themselves? Okay Mr. Davidson, I'll accept that there isn't enough money, but they mustn't expect me to try and get every operation done. If I don't have enough staff, then operations will be cancelled, the waiting list will be longer, and the patients will complain."

"Yes, well, that's the other thing. I've been instructed to tell you that they won't agree to a lot of operations being cancelled. And I'm sorry, but they don't want that information banded about. I'm sorry Katrina, you and your staff are going to have to work harder in future."

"Harder!" she exclaimed. "Have a look at the overtime book, why don't you?" and she handed the book to the couple. "You'll see how hard my staff and I work already. Most of us don't even make a note if we're only ten minutes late going off duty, such as last night, when I didn't get off duty until gone half past five, and I haven't claimed for it."

Ian Davidson looked upset. "I did try and persuade them otherwise" he said, but Katrina didn't care anymore. "How many new medical staff have they allowed to be appointed then?" she said. "I notice there is no shortage of doctors. Okay Dr. Davidson, I'll tell my staff what you've said, tell them that the committee expects them to work harder, and see what happens. If we all go off sick at once, then perhaps the committee will agree that we need more staff."

Miss Betts had been silent through this conversation, but now she joined in. "I did tell you, Dr. Davidson, that I will be restricting the surgeons to two large operations per list. I need to look after my staff, and I would be failing in my duty to them, if I didn't make sure that they are not overworked. But I'm warning you, if any of my staff have to go on sick leave because of overwork, then I will be going to see the committee myself. We're not finished with this." and she got up from her chair, and walked to the door. Still apologising to Katrina, Ian Davidson followed her, and the two of them left her alone. She looked up as there was a knock on the door, and Bella and Anne walked in. "What was all that about?" Anne demanded. Dr. Davidson wouldn't talk to any of us, and Miss Betts looked as though she was gearing herself for a battle."

"She is" Katrina said. "The committee have told them that there isn't any money to appoint any more staff, and if anybody else leaves, then the position won't be filled. They've confirmed that they won't pay us overtime, and we've got to take time in lieu. They've said we've got to work harder in future."

"Harder?" Anne demanded. "How can we work any harder than we do at the moment?"

"They just want to kill us all with overwork" Bella said and Anne agreed. Katrina sat back and listened to her staff nurses complaining about the decision, and then stopped them. "Miss Betts has told them that she's going to try and restrict the lists to two large cases per day, but I doubt if that's going to happen, and if any of her staff go off sick with overwork, then she's going to go and see the committee herself, and tell them what they've done. She reckons that she's not finished trying to help us."
"What did you say to Dr. Davidson?" Anne demanded. Katrina shrugged, "I showed him the overtime book, told him how much overtime we all worked now, but he said his hands were tied. Sorry girls, we're going to have to have a think about how we play this in future. Leave it with me for today, and I'll see what I can work out. But, don't tell the others, I'll get them together and tell them myself. If anybody is going to be blamed for this, then it's going to be me. As the senior person, then I'll be the unpopular one." Her two staff nurses disagreed, but Katrina was adamant, and although they didn't want her to take the full responsibility, they eventually agreed, and left her to finish the off duty. She sighed, and wondered how long it would take before the surgeons started complaining at Miss Betts edict about the length of the lists, and ignoring the limit in the number of large cases per day. She had been looking forward to the evening ahead, but with this problem hanging over her, she knew she might be distracted, and hoped Simon would understand that the situation wasn't of her making.

Her meeting with her other staff, was a re-run of her discussion with her senior nurses. They were all disgusted with what had been decided by the committee, but when Katrina told them they would be expected to work harder in future, the expressions on their faces showed what they thought about that. “We'll do all we can to help you Katrina” said Janet, “but you've got to remember, that we all have outside lives as well, and we can't always say we can stay late.”
“I know that, and remember that I've got a life outside as well,” Katrina said, “and hopefully I won't have to ask you to stay late too often. Miss Betts is on our side, and doesn't want any of us to go off sick with overwork, so if there's a problem with the surgeons not wanting to cancel patients, refer them to me, and I'll have to deal with it. They're only human, like us, and they won't want to work too hard either, and they should understand that we can only do what we can. I think I'm going to have to think about weekends as well. If we're going to be doing much more overtime, nobody is going to be able to take their time back, so I might put people on call over the weekend, instead of expecting them to come in and work. At least that way, you might be able to get some free time. I don't know what you think about that, would it be suit everybody?” She looked at the faces, and knew there were problems ahead. “Think about it” she said, “and let me know what you decide next week. Until then, I'm hoping we can sort out the lists and try and get them down to a decent level, without arguing too much with the surgeons. But just remember this, if you are in

charge in the evening, and the surgeons want to run on with their lists, the answer is definitely no, unless there are enough staff to cover their list, and the emergency list. And, in future, put all your overtime down, even if it's only ten or fifteen minutes. Let's show the committee how much overtime we all have to do to finish the lists. Thanks girls." She smiled at her staff, then dismissed them back to their theatres and went back to work.

That evening, as she waited for Simon to come and take her out, she thought back to her conversation with Miss Betts and Ian Davidson. They had appeared to be on her side, but she didn't know how much they would back her up, if she made the changes that seemed to be necessary. She sighed, and decided to forget about everything for tonight, as the doorbell rang, and she went to answer it, and greet the arrival of the man she liked and who she knew liked her.

Chapter Five

As she drove her Mini towards her parents' house, Katrina's mouth curved in a smile, as the memory of her evening out with Simon came back to her. They had gone to a restaurant not too far from her flat, and they had both enjoyed the meal. However, when he had taken her home, he had kissed her, and things had gone on from there, and the rest of the evening and night had been a pleasure to them both. He had stayed with her, unwilling to leave until the morning came, and the night had been a delight to her. He was a good and considerate lover, and she had enjoyed herself very much, as indeed had he. She had not wanted to go into the theatres that morning, but she had gone, knowing that she would see him again soon. He had kissed her goodbye, saying if he didn't see her in theatre that day, he would do his best to see her on Sunday evening, and she had known that he would do his best. He hadn't been able to see her during Friday, and she had gone home, before driving to her parents' home. Eleanor had visited theatre and asked her to give her love to her parents, but nothing else, and Katrina had agreed to do so. Now, she drew up outside the house she had been bought up in, got out of the car, and went to the front door. Her reunion with her parents was good, and she was glad to be able to see them again and looking so well after their extended holiday. Her mother had cooked a meal, and she was delighted when David arrived, just as they were about to sit down, but her mother had been expecting him, and had cooked enough food for him. The talk over the meal was of her parents' holiday, and how much they had enjoyed themselves and it was as she and David did the washing up afterwards, that she asked him what he wanted to talk to her about. "Come for a walk with me tomorrow, and I'll tell you," he said softly. "I want to ask your advice about something, before I talk to the parents. Do you know what time you're going home tomorrow?

"No," she had replied, remembering Simon's words. "But I'll go early, so you can have a chat with them in peace, without a third party being present, and also somebody wants to come and see me tomorrow evening."

"Oh, is this the person who took you out on Thursday?" he asked, with a smile, and she nodded. "Somebody special?" he asked, and she nodded again. "He could be" she said, "it seems good at the moment, but I'm hoping he feels the same way as I do. But I'll come for a walk with you tomorrow morning, if that's what you want."

"I do," he answered, "but I'll keep my fingers crossed for you" he said, as he dried the dishes, before they went back to talk to their parents.

As they walked through the woods near her parents' home, the following day, David began to talk. "I'm gay" was his abrupt opening line, and she nodded. "Yes, I know" she answered, and he stopped walking so abruptly, she had gone a few paces before she realised, he was no longer beside her. "How did you know?" he asked, when he caught up with her again, "and what do you think about it, and do you think Mum and Dad will be very upset."

"No" she said, decisively, answering his last question first, having thought about it since Simon had mentioned it. "I don't think they'll be upset. They will want you to be happy, and if you're going to be happy with somebody, then I can't see that they're going to be upset if it's male or female. And, I'm very happy that you've finally acknowledged it, David."

He smiled as she said this, "So, how did you know?" he asked again.

"My friend and I were talking one evening, and he mentioned the possibility, and we wondered if it was the case, and the more I thought about it, the more it seemed to fit."

"You've been talking about me" David said slowly, but Katy shook her head. "No, he just happened to mention something, and that's when we speculated about it. But we haven't talked any more about it since then, and certainly I've said nothing to anybody else. Things just seemed to add up, if you know what I mean. Nothing more than that. But it's nobody's business but yours, so don't let anything anybody says upset you. Actually, you've kept the secret very well" she smiled, "to have reached the age you are now, without telling anybody, I'm quite impressed. How long have you known?" He shrugged, "Years. I started thinking about the possibility when I was at school, but I didn't want to admit it to myself until I'd left medical school, and I was working as a house officer. I'd had female friends, but they didn't do anything for me, and I realised that I didn't want to be with a woman, I much preferred being with people of my own sex. I've had friends, but I hadn't met anybody I wanted to spend the rest of my life with, and I'd resigned myself to being alone. But about three years ago, I went to a conference and met my friend, who's a doctor as well, we kind of clicked, everything made sense and we've been together since then, and things have gone on from there." He smiled. "It's been a voyage of discovery, if you know what I mean? We obviously get on very well together, we're happy to be together when we can, and our friendship has got a lot deeper, but working in different hospitals and not having a lot of free time between us, it's sometimes been difficult, which is why we were thinking of moving in together, if we can. And that is the reason why I thought I'd better tell everybody. But I wanted to tell you, before I told anybody else. You and I have always been close, haven't we?" She nodded, "Yes, sometimes I feel closer to you, than I do to Eleanor, and we're meant to be twins. Does he have a name, this friend of yours?"

"Yes," David replied with a smile, "but as you're not going to tell me your friends name, then I am not going to tell you mine. One day, I hope I can introduce you to him. But I hope you're going to be happy with your friend Katy. If he upsets you, let me know and I'll beat him up."

"And what if he's bigger than you?" she said with a grin, but David shrugged. "I'll take him out for a drink, and let him know what I think about him." She grinned at him, knowing that he and Simon were exactly the same size. "Thank you for telling me, and I won't tell anybody else, you know that. Just be happy Dave, and when you want to, introduce him to me and the rest of the family" she said. "I know everybody will be happy for you." She reached up and gave him a hug. "Thanks Katy", he responded, and they continued walking, talking about other things.

As she drove back towards her flat on that Sunday afternoon, she wondered if Simon would be able to visit her. She didn't want to telephone him, to find out, just in case Eleanor was nearby when he answered, but decided to bleep her sister and tell her of her visit. When her sister answered, she asked if she were busy, and on being told that she wasn't, she passed on the messages from her parents, and told her sister she would see her on the following day. "Have you got any idea of what Simon's got on his list tomorrow?" she asked, wondering whether she would have to tell him he couldn't do all his cases. "Not a lot" Eleanor said, "as far as I know, there are two laparotomies, and a couple of small ones, closure of a colostomy I think, and something else."
"Okay" Katrina said. "See you tomorrow" and she replaced the receiver. She was in the bedroom, unpacking her overnight bag, when Simon phoned to see if she were home, and he arrived that evening, as she was making a snack meal, for she had eaten a meal at lunchtime with her parents, and she was delighted to see him again. His greeting was all she wanted, and she gave herself up to the pleasure of being in his arms again. His mouth was hard on hers, as they kissed and kissed again. "Have you been busy?" she asked after their first greetings, but he

shook his head. “I've only done one case all day” he answered. “If you do decide to put the staff on call for the weekend, then they would have been able to get some rest.”
“How did you know about that?” she asked, for she hadn't been able to tell him on Thursday, and he grinned at her. “Bella told me, while she was scrubbed with me this afternoon” he replied. “She also told me what Ian Davidson said, she was fuming about it, and I don't blame her. It's not fair on you girls, and I shall tell him if I get the chance.”
“It's not his fault” Katrina said, “he's only told us what the committee have said. He told us that he put the case for more staff to them, but they didn't listen.”
“I wonder how strongly he put the case?” he wondered, then bent and kissed her again. “Don't worry Katy, I'll be good and not put too many cases on the list.”
“I realised over the weekend that we can't do on calls anyway. If you get an emergency aneurysm in, we'd only have 10 minutes or less, to be able to lay up, and none of the staff would be able to get in, in time. We're going to have to work the duty. Anyway, that's my problem. What have you put on tomorrow?” she asked. “When I spoke to Elly, she said you'd got two laparotomies and two small cases.”
“Yes” he answered. “That sounds right. But we're not going to talk about work tonight. How was your weekend?” She grinned up at him “Remember what you told me what you thought about David? Well, you were right. He and I had a talk this morning, and

he wanted to know what I thought about how mum and dad would take it. He has got a special friend, but wouldn't tell me who it was." She leaned up and kissed him, then grinned again. "Mind you, I wouldn't tell him who my special friend was, so I suppose we were even." Simon smiled as he kissed her. "We'll keep everything a secret, shall we? It's not that I don't want to acknowledge you, but it could be difficult working together if we are a pair. Of course," .... he broke off, and wouldn't say anything else, just held her tight against him and kissed her again, so she forgot what she was about to say. They spent an enjoyable evening together, but he wouldn't stay the night, because he was on call, and didn't want to disturb her, if he was called out. When he left her that evening, she felt very lonely, but knew that she would see him on the following day.

When she went into work on Monday, she looked at the lists and found that only Simon had kept his to a decent level, and knew that the girls were going to be asked to stay on to finish them. The worst culprit of all was Darren James, who had caused the original problem, and when he came in to the theatre unit, she immediately called him into the office to discuss his list. "So which cases do you want to cancel now?" she asked him. He looked surprised and answered "None of them. I need to get them all done today."
"There is no way you will finish this list" she said firmly. "I am telling you now, that at least one, and possibly two, of these cases will have to be

cancelled."
"I believe Ian Davidson told you that the committee don't want too many cases to be cancelled" he said with a smirk, and suddenly Katrina knew that he was one of the committee who weren't allowing extra staff to be appointed. "And how would you know that Mr. James?" she said quietly, "unless of course, you are on the committee." He had the grace to look ashamed and she knew she was right. "You have made the members of staff in this department very unhappy about the way you are refusing to let anybody else be appointed here. We simply don't have enough staff to be able to manage" she said quietly, not wanting to have an argument with him. "My staff and I work very hard to try and make sure that none of the patients are cancelled, but as we are only human, and we have their own lives to lead. I am not willing to let my staff make themselves ill, in order to suit you, or any of the other surgeons. Why don't you think about anybody else when you are making out your operating lists?"
"Don't you try and lecture me Sister" he blustered. "I'll put as many cases on my lists as I feel able to do myself, and if your staff can't cope with them, then I suggest they find another job." He turned and walked away from her, and she shook her head, mentally redoing the work list, so that there were enough staff to cover him. Katrina went back into the office, and looked at the lists. They were going to be short of staff again that evening, so if Sally, the late staff nurse covered Mr. James list, that would leave one nurse and an auxiliary to do the emergency list. She hoped that there would be enough

anaesthetic staff to cover that list, and assist the auxiliary, otherwise the emergency list would be delayed, and that would annoy the other surgeons. She picked up the off-duty book, to take it into theatre with her, to work on while she looked after Janet, who was going to do the main case in Theatre Two. She had said hello to Simon when he came in, but when he asked her if she was going to scrub for him, she had shaken her head. "Why not?" he asked, and then grinned as she looked pointedly at his hands. "I think you know why" she smiled at him. "Fine" he whispered, "I'll see you tomorrow." and he had gone out of the office.

By the time she had finished her list, and the other cases were coming to an end, Darren James list was still going on. She had gone into the theatre to find out where they were and been disgusted to find there were still two cases to go, one of them quite a long case. "Where's Sally?" she had asked the auxiliary, meaning the other member of the late staff. "We thought she was with you" Theresa said quietly. "We haven't seen her at all."
"Has anybody heard anything from her" she asked, but nobody knew what had happened. She went back into the coffee room, and addressed the members of staff who were there. "Anybody seen Sally, or heard from her?" she asked, but everybody shook their heads. She had gone back into the theatre, when Mr James raised his head. "Did I hear you ask where Sally is?" he asked, and she nodded. "Yes. Have you heard anything?"
"Oh, didn't I tell you?" he said mockingly, "she

phoned in, and said she won't be in today. She's not well."

"And didn't it occur to you to tell me? After all, I am the senior person in this theatre." she said. "Well, that settles it. I'm sorry, but you are not going to be able to carry on and do your lists. I'll phone the wards and tell them to feed the patients."

"You won't do anything of the sort" he insisted. "I need to operate on those patients. I'm not cancelling them."

"There aren't the staff to do the list, as Sally isn't available to scrub for you" she insisted. "You would have a runner nurse, but no scrub nurse."

"Well, why can't you stay?" he asked, and she gave him a nasty look. "Why should I?" she asked. "I wouldn't get paid for it, I wouldn't be able to take the extra time back, and I'm giving enough of my life to these operating theatres as it is." She was standing by the side of the operating table as she spoke to the surgeon, and looked up to see her sister standing in the doorway. Eleanor had been scrubbed for Simon that day, but she was on call again, and was preparing to take over from Darren James SHO.

"Oh, go on Sister" she urged. "The patients are ready for surgery. We can't cancel them now."

"We can and we will, and stop trying to interfere with my running of the theatres." Katrina said, but her sister smiled at her. "Please, Sister, stay late to do just one case."

"And how long is it going to take?" she asked. Mr. James smirked at her, knowing she was weakening. "It shouldn't be longer than an hour or so."

"I will try and get the Neuro. or the Ortho. staff to

come and assist you." she said. "I am not going to stay late again." and she walked out of the room. Simon came up to her as she allowed the doors to swing shut behind her. "What's the problem?" he asked, "Darren James wanting to run over again?" She nodded "And Eleanor. She's just asked me why I can't stay to finish the list. He's got two more cases to do, didn't bother to tell me that Sally won't be in, and won't let me cancel any of the patients. I've just got to go and phone the other theatres to see if they can let me borrow somebody who can come and do the case." she glanced around but there was nobody within earshot, "I've found out that he's on the committee," she murmured, "he told me this morning, when I told him that the list was too long, that Ian Davidson had told us that he didn't want us to cancel too many patients, and the only way he'd have known that, was if he'd been a member of the committee. Ian had told Miss Betts and myself, that he wasn't going to make that common knowledge." She pushed herself tiredly, away from the wall she had been leaning on, before going to walk to the office. Simon accompanied her, and stayed when she made the phone calls. Luckily, one of the orthopaedic staff on a late duty, had general surgical experience and was willing to assist, but she knew that if there not had been anybody available, then she would have had to stay. "I'll see you tomorrow" he whispered, as she went to get changed, and she smiled at him, thankful that he didn't want to see her that evening, for she was very tired, and was looking forward to an early night.

From that day on, things seemed to go from bad to worse. Darren James made his lists longer and longer, and the other surgeons decided that as he was able to get away with it, they made their lists longer as well. He wouldn't allow any cases to be cancelled if they were running over time, there often weren't any nurses who were able to take over from the early staff, and more often than not, it was Katrina who had to stay late to finish the list. Ian Davidson didn't come and ask her if she had enough staff to be able to cope, and she knew he was avoiding her. She began to lose weight, get dark marks under her eyes, and the amount of overtime she accrued grew larger, day by day. She began to long for Tuesdays and Thursdays when she was sometimes able to see Simon, for he was not on call on those days, and he had several weekends free, but because there weren't enough staff to cover, Katrina often had to work. Her staff were working as hard, but as the senior nurse, it was her responsibility. Eleanor seemed to enjoy winding her sister up, and Katrina was often hard pushed to stop snapping at her twin when she suggested she should stay late, or work more overtime. Christmas had come and gone, and as Simon had been on duty, they hadn't been busy, and she had been grateful for that, for she knew that if Darren James had been due to work, she would have needed call in more staff to cover the cases he would want to do. "That can be your Christmas present" he said, when she thanked him for not working, and grinned at her, for he had given her a present already. It was nearly time for Eleanor to leave Simon's team and go to work for

Ewan Dexter, for his lists weren't as long as some, and Katrina was thankful, for her sister had not made her job very easy, trying to ingratiate herself with the other surgeons. One evening, when neither of them were needed at the hospital, Katrina was relaxing with Simon. He had cooked her a meal, worried about her lack of energy, and they were sitting on the settee with a glass of wine, just talking about things in general, when Simon told her he was being sent to a conference the following week. "I'm going next Monday morning, and I hope to be back on the Friday evening, 10 days later, so I won't be seeing you for nearly two weeks" he said, kissing her gently. "I thought I'd be able to get out of going, but the committee have told me I've got to go. And worse than that, I've got to take an SHO with me. They want me to take Eleanor, as she's my SHO." Katrina sat up straight, and stared at him. "But surely she'll be moving to Ewan Dexter's team by then." He shook his head. "Hasn't she told you? The committee want her to stay with me for another three months, to get more experience of my major arterial work." Katrina groaned. "She's going to love that, but she's going to make it more difficult for us to be together." Simon leaned forward and kissed her gently. "You know I only want to be with you" he said. "Katy, darling Katy, don't you realise that I need you, I want to spend all my time with you." he kissed her gently, then a lot harder, and they ended up lying in each other's arms on the settee. "So where are you going for this conference?" she asked him, when she had recovered her breath and he grinned at her. "Would you believe, Amsterdam?" he

said, and she groaned. “I've always wanted to go there” she said, “You don't need a scrub nurse to come with you instead of an SHO do you?”
“Sorry darling, I'd take you with me in a heartbeat, but the committee are insisting on an SHO.” He kissed her again, “I’ll take you there one day, just us two, but don't worry my darling, I'll be true to you, I won't look at anybody else, I'll try and phone every day, and I'll bring you back a present.” They kissed again, before he looked at her quizzically. “Do you have any preference for colour?” he asked, and she looked quizzically at him. “What for?” she asked, and he smiled. “I wondered what your favourite colour was.” he said. “We've never really talked about things like that, so I don't know your preferences.” She thought for a minute, then smiled. “I like green” she said. “I've got quite a few green clothes; it doesn't clash with my hair or anything like that. I can't wear red, and blue doesn't really suit me.”
“I'll remember that.” he said, then kissed her again. “Don't let Darren James upset you while I'm away” he said. “He's trying to wind you up whenever he can. And Katy, you've got to eat properly while I'm away. You've lost more weight, and it doesn't suit you.”
“I do eat” she retorted. “But Darren James needs to be talked to severely by management. He's a complete nightmare, and because he's a senior consultant, the other surgeons seem to think his attitude is the correct one, and they follow his lead. Miss Betts did try to tell them that we could only do two major cases on each list, but they seem to have forgotten all about that now.” she sighed. “I really

don't like the man, and he does his best to upset me. He is urging the other surgeons to put more cases on their lists, tells them not to let us cancel them, and the anaesthetists won't listen to us now. Even Ian Davidson isn't asking if we're okay now. Honest Simon, if we don't get more staff, then somebody is going to go off sick, and there's going to be more pressure on the rest of us. We've lost Emma, and we knew Simone was going, and we don't even have students now who we can train, who could take some of the pressure off of us. That's his fault as well. He told the teaching staff that he didn't think it was correct to send us students when we were so busy, and they listened to him, despite everything that Miss Betts said."

He leant forward, took her into his arms and held her close. "Try not to think about it." he murmured, as he kissed her again, "Think about this instead" and he caressed her body kissing her deeply as he did so. "I'll phone you from the conference every night I can, and you can tell me what's been happening. But Joe Davis won't be doing very many big cases on my list, while I'm away, so you won't have to worry about them. You'll be able to have an easy day on the days when I'm meant to be operating." She grinned, "Thank goodness" she muttered. "Are you on call this weekend, you did tell me, but I've forgotten."

"No" he said. "And I hope you're not working either."

"Well, I'm not meant to be, but if anybody goes off sick, then I might have to cover."

"No, you're not going to cover." he was adamant about that. "You did the on call last weekend

because Janet was off sick, so you can't do another one. How long is it since you had a day off, and didn't have to go in?"
"Thirteen days" she admitted, and he sat up in shock. "Katy, you can't keep on like this. You'll be ill, if you're not careful. You've got to take a couple of days off, and get right away from this place. I'll take you away for the weekend, I think. Now, where do you fancy going? Shall we go to the Cotswolds?" He kissed her again, and she kissed him back. "I'd like that" she said tiredly. "But don't book anything will you, just in case I have to work."
"I told you; you're not going to work." he was getting angry now. "You need a break. You've got a perfectly good team, and I'm sure one of them would take over for you if necessary. I'll book a hotel, and we can go on Friday afternoon, straight after work." She nodded and gave in. "Okay" she said. "I'll let Bella know that I won't be available if there's a problem."
"Good girl" he said, and kissed her. "I'm not staying tonight" he said, "I've got a big case tomorrow, so I'll need to concentrate on it, but I'll come and see you on Thursday. Are you going to scrub for me tomorrow, or are you putting somebody else on to do it?"
"I've put Janet on, but if she's still not feeling too well, then I'll have to do it. Have you got anything else on the list or is that it?"
"No, only the one case. You won't have to stay late tomorrow night for me to finish."
"Good" she muttered, and kissed him. He kissed her gently, then harder, and they ended up laying

together and embracing each other closely, caressing each other as they did so. At last, he broke the kiss, put her away from him, and stood up. "Goodnight darling. See you tomorrow", then he kissed her again, before he left her. As he left the building, he didn't know he was being observed. Eleanor had come to visit her sister, but had seen Simon's car, and wanting to know who he was visiting, she had stayed where she was. She saw Simon leaving the building, and several things fitted together suddenly. Now she knew who he was seeing, she thought, and realising why he had not reacted to her, when she had tried her best to get him interested in her. She never normally had any problem in getting men interested in her, but Simon had been difficult. She watched him drive away, decided not to call on Katrina, and instead walked back to the hospital, deep in thought. She knew she was going to be going to Holland with Simon, and wondered if she could think of something to upset her sister while she was away.

Katrina had packed a weekend case, told her staff she was not available, no matter what happened in the theatres, turned her mobile phone off so nobody could contact her, and was ready and waiting for Simon when he arrived at her flat at lunchtime on Friday. He greeted her with a kiss, picked up her case, and took it downstairs, loading it into the car, while Katrina locked up and followed him downstairs. "Ready?" he asked, and she nodded. "Where are we going?" she asked, and he grinned. "I'm taking you to Stow on the Wold, I've booked a hotel there, and I'm going to make sure that you have a lovely relaxing weekend." He bent his head, kissed her again, and they set off. The drive to the town took them quite a while, for there was a lot of traffic around, but when they arrived, she was entranced by the hotel. It was on the High Street, quite old, but very luxurious, and she knew she was going to be happy that weekend. And so, it proved. Simon was a good escort, took her for dinner that evening, and as they sat over their meal, he poured her another glass of wine. "I'm not going to be driving anywhere tonight" he said, as he poured one for himself as well. "We can just relax and enjoy ourselves." She enjoyed herself immensely, not having to worry about finding staff for the theatres, just enjoying herself being with him. She knew deep in her heart that she loved him, and although she wanted to tell him so, she found herself unable to do so. He had never said anything to her, about loving her, and she didn't want to spoil the good relationship she had with him, by asking him his feelings. That night, she slept well, cradled in his arms, and when Simon woke her with a long kiss in the morning, she felt much refreshed. After a leisurely breakfast, they went for a walk in the town, stopping to stare into shop windows, before he took her for a drive around the surrounding countryside, and onto a restaurant in a nearby large town, where they ate Italian food, and relaxed as they talked. "I'll be able to come and see you on Tuesday, and Thursday." he said, and she knew he would do his best to do that. "I'm on call at the weekend, bad planning on my part, but I haven't been able to change my on call, and as I've got to get everything ready for going away on Monday, I don't think I'll be able to come and see you on Sunday evening."

"I'm working anyway on the weekend so we'll see each other if you have to operate" she said, and he shook his head. "Why do you have to do all the weekends?" he asked. "Surely, some of your staff would be able to work? Why is it always left to you?"

She sat back and concentrated on her plate. "Because they'd already requested the weekend off, and there isn't anybody else who can deal with things. I'd already said that I'd do the weekend anyway. Honest Simon, it's not only my theatres that are being affected by the committee's decisions. Orthopaedics in particular have been very badly affected, and they're losing at least two more staff on maternity leave in a couple of months' time, so goodness knows how they're going to cope." she sighed, "Perhaps by then, the committee will have decided that we need some more nurses, and allow us to advertise. But somehow, I don't think they will do, unless something drastic happens."

He put his hand over hers, "Forget it for tonight" he said, "I'll take you back to the hotel now, and we can talk about other things, and you can have good night's sleep again. Last night you slept very well, which just goes to prove that you needed it. Don't worry little Katy, things will get better soon." and she loved him even more than she did, for his words.

The following day, they went to morning service in the large church in the town, and then went on to an antiques fair, they had seen advertised. She was entranced by the goods on sale, and although Simon wanted to buy her a present, she refused. “I don't know what I want” she said, “so there's no point in buying anything that I might not like in a couple of months or so.” She leant up and kissed him on the cheek. “But thank you for thinking of me.” At that, he took her in his arms, and kissed her very deeply. “I'll always think of you” he said, when he lifted his head, and she felt so very happy.

The drive back to his house was achieved quite quickly, and as she cuddled close to him that night, he held her close to him, hugging her tight, and kissing her deeply. “Thank you for my weekend” she said, “I had a really great time, and you were right, I did need to get away from the hospital completely.” He kissed her again, and started to caress her, and before she lost all sense, she knew she was exactly where she wanted to be. The next morning, when he drove her back to her flat, so that they could go their separate ways into work, she knew she was going to miss him when he had to go away, and tried, but failed, to push down the flare of envy that she felt, at her sister, who was going to go with him.

Chapter Six

Simon and Eleanor had gone away to Holland to their conference, and Katrina was missing him dreadfully. He had phoned her a couple of times, once when they had arrived, and again the evening of the second day, but since then, she had heard nothing, but she admitted to herself, she had been very busy. She had tried phoning him, but it had gone straight to voicemail, so she knew he was probably very busy himself. The theatres were as busy as ever, but any hope that Simon's lists would be quieter, had been scotched by Darren James, who had informed Joe, Simon's registrar, that he was going to use them, to clear some of his backlog. It had been gone 7.30 pm when Katrina had left on Monday and Tuesday evenings, and nearly 8.00 pm on the Wednesday and Thursday, and the following week, she knew would probably be just as bad. She had asked Joe on the Friday evening, why he had allowed it, but although he had apologised, he had told her he had been unable to resist. "He is my ultimate boss, you know. Although I'm working for Simon, its ultimately Mr. James who can make or break my career, and as I'm working hard to get my exams, I don't want to have to worry about upsetting him. I'm sorry Katrina, honest I am. But Simon will be home the week after next, and you won't have to worry about his lists over running. You know how careful he is, not to expect you to work late to finish the list." he grinned at her. "He phoned yesterday, told me to make sure that there's only one case on his list for the week he comes back, but it's going to be another big arterial one, so it will be an all day one. He asked if you'd be able to scrub for it?" Katrina had murmured in answer, and gone to the office. Why hadn't Simon phoned her, she wondered? He had said he would phone every day, and although he'd been gone nearly five days, she'd only heard from him twice. She walked back to the theatre after going to talk to the CSSD about missing instruments, in a very nasty mood – a bad mood increased by the fact that she was going to have to work the weekend again. Bella had developed a stomach upset, and couldn't come back to work, while there was a danger of passing it on to the other members of staff. Nobody had been available to cover the sickness absence, so it had been left to Katrina to do so. "Another fourteen-day stretch" she muttered to herself, as she walked home that evening, hoping that Simon would phone her that evening. When the phone rang, she seized it, but it was only her brother, David wanting to know how she was, and keeping her up to date with family developments, and when she put the phone down again, she knew that she was very upset that Simon hadn't phoned. There had, however, been a postcard from him on the doormat, and she had read it with a smile. He couldn't say much, just said he missed her, and was looking forward to seeing her again. She carefully put it under her pillow before she went to bed that night, and slept with her hand touching it. The weekend was busy – Darren James was on call, and although the patients weren't emergencies, he had decided that they needed surgery immediately, and she was to tired to argue with him. When she finally got home at 5.30 on Sunday evening, having had to stay and work on what was meant to be a half day, she couldn't be bothered to cook, as indeed she hadn't been bothering to cook for the past week, instead having several cups of tea, and a sandwich. But as she hadn't been able to go shopping, there was very little food in the fridge anyway! By the time Friday came around, she was very, very tired. She had had to work overtime every day, hadn't managed to take her half day, and hadn't left the department until at least six thirty on every evening. Her lunch breaks had been a quick 15 minutes if she was lucky. She had worked non-stop all week, hadn't been able to take any time back, and desperately needed a day off, and was looking forward to the following day, when she would be able to leave the department behind, and hopefully, see Simon. She was called to see Miss Betts in the afternoon, and didn't see the long look that the other woman gave her, until she was told to sit down while they discussed the problems in theatre. As she was about to leave, the older woman said gently, "Katrina my dear, you look worn out" she said. "How long has it been since you had a day off?"

"Fourteen days" she answered "I'm off tomorrow, hopefully, so I'll be able to have a rest then." The Nursing Officer shook her head. "It's not good enough. We just don't have enough staff. I've tried to make an appointment to see the committee." she told her, "But I've been told that they aren't meeting for a couple of weeks. I've seen the operating books, and I know how much overtime you are all having to

do. I'm sorry my dear, this situation can't go on much longer. All my senior staff look worn out, but you look as though you're on your last legs. How much overtime have you worked this month?"
Katrina shrugged. "Quite a bit" she answered. "I don't know exactly how much, but we definitely need some more staff."
"I've got some bad news for you, as well. I'm sorry Katrina, but Janet handed in her notice this morning. Her husband is being moved by his company, so you're going to be another staff member down. Are you going to be able to cope?"
"Probably not" she replied, knowing that this was the final straw. "And if anybody else goes, then we definitely won't be able to, and goodness knows how we're going to cope whenever anybody wants to book holidays. When you do manage to get to see the committee, ask them to come and see how hard we work in theatres, and see for themselves what their decision not to appoint more staff, is doing to us." She grinned tiredly at the other woman. "Let me loose on them, and I'll tell them." Miss Betts smiled back, worried at the lack of colour in Katrina's face, and the deep bags under her eyes. "Let me know if you desperately need help" she said, "and I'll see what I can do. Take care, and have a good weekend off won't you." Katrina left the office, wondering what Miss Betts would do, if she told her that she couldn't cope any more. The older woman wouldn't be able to magic up more staff, so there was no point in letting her know how short of staff they really were. And people were wanting to book holidays, but there was no way they would be able to

cope, when her staff took annual leave. She got back to her office, and stared at the pile of paperwork that needed attention. She really couldn't give it the attention it deserved, and swept it into a drawer of the desk, to deal with it later. She had left the hospital, and gone to her flat, laying in a hot bath, trying to relax, before deciding what to eat, but she couldn't relax properly, so washed her hair, allowing it to dry naturally, and leaving it loose round her shoulders, and curled up on the settee, to think. Simon should be home that evening, he had told her he hoped to see her tonight, but she'd only had two phone calls from him, and one postcard, and wondered if he was alright. She meant to have something to eat and drink, but instead drifted into a tired sleep, from which she awoke hours later, and deciding that he wasn't going to phone her tonight, she went to bed.

The ringing phone woke her, and she leapt from the bed to answer it, as she looked at the clock. It was 3.00 a.m., and she knew exactly what the phone call meant. The theatres needed staff, and they had phoned her to be able to get it. One of the night staff nurses spoke, almost as soon as she picked up the receiver. "Sister, oh thank goodness. We've got so many casualties, we need help."
"Calm down Susie" she spoke calmly, "What's the problem?"
"There's been a multiple pile up on the motorway, we're the nearest hospital, and we've got loads of casualties. The orthopaedic theatres are fully staffed, as they've all been called in, and now, we

desperately need some help. Can you come in please?" There was only one answer and Katrina gave it. "Of course," she said now. "I'll get dressed and come in. Get the theatres ready, and phone everybody else, apart from Kate and Emma. They're on in the morning, so they might as well have some rest until they are due in." She replaced the receiver, after hearing Susie agree, and went swiftly to get dressed. When she arrived in the theatres, the place was in uproar. Three consultant surgeons were waiting for a scrub nurse, so they could start operating, and she swiftly allocated staff to the theatres. It was nearly three pm the following afternoon, when she was able to get some of the staff off duty, for they had been working through the night, and everybody was tired. She didn't get off duty herself, until at least a couple of hours later, and went home, and straight to bed. She was called in the following day, as well, because the regular staff were operating and they desperately needed to open a second theatre to try and save the life of one of the accident victims, and by the time she got home, she was too tired to eat. Simon hadn't phoned her, although she had thought that she'd heard a phone ringing, but she had lain down and was asleep before she could think about it.

When she went into work the following day, she was really looking forward to seeing Simon again, but his list was full of small cases, which Joe and Eleanor could cope with, and there was no sign of him. She had agreed to do his list on her own, without another scrub nurse, as she had been told it

would be one of the big arterial cases, and she only needed an auxilliary to run for her for that, so worked through the day, without managing to get a full lunch break, or a coffee break. It was as she was coming back from the recovery room after she had taken the last patient there, that she finally managed to ask Joe where he was. "Did he get back from the conference okay?" she asked. "After all, Dr. Howard is here, and I thought they were going together."
"Yes," Joe agreed. "They went together, but Eleanor came back on her own. Simon was asked to go to Utrecht to do one of his special cases, and he agreed. He's hoping to be back on Thursday. In the meantime, I'll do as many of his small cases as I can, and leave the big ones for him, when he gets back. I'd already told Darren James he wasn't going to be able to use the lists for his own cases." He took a good look at her, and frowned. "Katrina, are you alright? You look whacked, and I swear you've lost some more weight."
"I'm fine" she said. "I've been working hard recently, so maybe that's why I'm not eating as much as I should."
"It doesn't suit you" he said. "Why not come to dinner with Sarah and myself. I'm not on call tonight, and as you were here early, you won't be required to stay late. Sarah was asking me why she hasn't seen you for a while, just last week."
"Joe, I'd love to come" Katrina said earnestly, "if you're sure it won't upset Sarah."
"Of course not." he smiled. "Give me half an hour to make sure that the patients are okay, and let Sarah know you're coming to dinner, I'll get changed, and

then I'll take you home with me."
"Okay" she said. "Let me get changed, and make sure that everybody is okay, and I'll be waiting for you outside." She went into the other theatres, to find out how they were doing, and deciding that everybody was coping well, she went to get changed to go and meet Joe. It was a pity, that just after she walked out of the unit, the phone rang, and Eleanor picked it up, to find Simon on the other end. "Is Sister Howarth there?" he asked, but Eleanor knew this was another opportunity to make mischief. "No" she said quickly. "She's already gone. I heard her making arrangements to go out with somebody tonight, so I don't think she'll be at her home either." Simon shook his head. He had been trying to get in touch with Katrina for days now – her mobile phone had been out of charge for a few days, she was never in when he tried the land line, and he wondered who she was going out with tonight. "Okay, thanks Eleanor. You managed to get home okay; I take it?"
"Yes," she said. "The flight was okay and today's list went off okay. Joe did a few of the smaller cases that needed to be done."
"Okay" he said. "I'm hoping to be back on Thursday evening, so I'll see you then." and he replaced the receiver.

Katrina enjoyed having a meal with Joe and Sarah. She had been friends with Sarah for a long time, since she arrived at the hospital, and married Joe, and when she had left to have a baby, she and Katrina had remained good friends. "So, how's your love life" Sarah asked her when they had finished

eating, but Katrina wasn't going to tell her the truth. "Okay" she answered, "nothing permanent, if you know what I mean, just enjoying each other's companionship."
"Who is it?" she was asked, but Katrina shook her head. "Nobody you'd know" she said, with a grin, and surreptitiously crossed her fingers, because Sarah did indeed know Simon. "Joe told me how hard you've been working lately" Sarah said. "Actually Katy, you look terrible. You look very tired."
"I'm not sleeping too well, and of course, we're having to work a lot harder than usual, because the surgeons are putting more cases on their lists, and we're all having to work overtime. The committee decided we'd got enough staff, they won't let us appoint any more, and we can't replace people who leave. If they don't rescind that last order quite quickly, then there is going to be trouble. Janet's handed her notice in, because her husband is being moved, and when she goes in three weeks time, we won't have enough staff to cover the lists, and if anybody goes off sick, the rest of us are going to suffer. We're all doing loads of overtime, and we don't stand a chance of getting any of it back." Sarah nodded. She had been a theatre nurse before she married, and knew what Katrina meant. "It's not funny anymore. Miss Betts is doing her level best to try and change everybody's minds, but with people like Darren James on the committee, it's going to be difficult."
"Is he on the committee?" Sarah asked, and Joe looked very surprised. "How on earth did you find

that out?" he asked, and Katrina smiled wryly. "Oh, he made a comment about us not cancelling the patients, and as Ian Davidson had told us that he was keeping that a secret, so the only people who would have known, were committee members. And when I told him that, and asked him if he was on the committee, he looked a bit ashamed. I expect Joe told you how he took over Simon Parker's lists last week, and we all had to work lots of overtime to get them done."

"So how much overtime have you done lately?" Sarah looked concerned, but Katrina just laughed at her. "I'd need a calculator to work it out. It's a lot, and I don't stand a chance of getting any of it back." she said. "I know I need a day off, because I haven't had one for a while." Sarah shook her head. "Katy, you can't go on like this. You need a few days off. You'll be ill, if you're not careful." she said firmly, but Katrina shook her head. "I can't take days off when we've got patients dying around us, and that motorway crash was almost the last straw, but as we don't have enough staff to be able to take time back, we don't have a choice. You know what it's like Sarah?" Her friend nodded and changed the subject, but later that evening, after Joe had taken Katrina back to her flat, and they were alone, she rounded on her husband. "Why are you lot allowing Darren James to be such a complete bastard to the staff?" she asked. "You must have seen how tired Katy looked tonight. I've never seen her look so bad. She's lost so much weight as well. Her clothes are absolutely hanging on her. And who's she going out with? Can't he help?"

"I have absolutely no idea who it is." he replied. "Honest Sarah, I didn't realise how bad things were. Remember we don't see her in outdoor clothing, and theatre scrubs can hide a multitude of sins, as you well know, but I think I'm going to have to have a talk to Simon when he gets back, and ask him what can be done. He's the only consultant keeping his lists to a decent level, and a couple of the other registrars, have said that the committee decision is unfair on the girls, but none of us can challenge it. We're all too junior to somebody like Darren James. It needs somebody with a lot more clout than a registrar." He gave Sarah a hug, and then hurriedly changed the subject.

The patient that Simon had operated upon in Utrecht made a really fast recovery, and Simon was able to go home, sooner than he had thought. He had not been able to contact Katy again, for she had been home late on Tuesday and he had been at the airport, having managed to get a seat on the late-night flight. He came out of the airport, after collecting his luggage, and was looking out for a taxi, when he bumped straight into David, who had been seeing some friends off after they had stayed with him. "David Howarth!" he said, and Katrina's brother shook his hand. "What the hell are you doing here?" Simon asked, "leaving the country?" David laughed at his friend's comment. "Just seeing some friends onto their plane." he said. "I could ask you the same thing" David asked, but Simon shook his head. "I've been in Utrecht, operating, and managed to get the last plane home tonight. I was just about to phone for a taxi, because I didn't leave my car here, but there don't seem to be any about."

"Don't bother" David said, "come and stay with me overnight, then you can get back to your house bright and early tomorrow. In fact, I've got to go to Queens tomorrow. I'm seeing one of your consultants about a trial we want to get involved with, and something else as well, so I'll drive you over, if you can wait until after lunch."

"I'd love to thanks. We can catch up on what's been happening in our lives since we were at med. school." He grinned at his friend. "You could come up to theatres and see how Katy is doing at the same time. Surprise her with a quick visit." David nodded, "Good idea. How is she lately? I spoke to her a couple of weeks ago, but I haven't seen her since we were at home together – must be about 8 weeks ago."

"She's working hard" Simon said. "I've been trying to get hold of her for a couple of weeks, since I was sent to the conference, but she's never in."

"Why have you been trying to get hold of her?" David asked, then grinned, "or are you the person whose name she wouldn't give me, when I asked her what the name of the special one was?"

"Well, I hope I'm the special one" Simon said "Any objections?" David shook his head. "No, good luck to her. At least I won't have to beat you up to make sure you treat her right." They both laughed at his comments, they had reached David's car now, and in the bustle of getting the luggage into the boot, and doing up seat belts, the subject was dropped.

Wednesday's list, for once, wasn't too heavy, although Katrina was doing it on her own, and because of that, she hadn't managed to get a lunch break or stop for a drink, and it was in the afternoon just before she was due to go home, that Eleanor approached her as she tidied the desk. They were in the office, and the door was open. Eleanor had continued talking about work. "Mr. James needs to finish his list" she said "Are you going to be able to scrub for him? He needs a senior person to be able to stay and do the case." Katrina shook her head. "No." she said slowly. "For once there are enough senior staff to stay and scrub for him. I'm going to go home." She looked at Eleanor and changed the subject. "So how was Amsterdam?" Eleanor smiled widely, "oh it was great" she gushed, and Katrina knew her sister was going to elaborate on her answer. She didn't trust her sister when she spoke in that manner. "They looked after us so well, made sure that the hotel we were in, was in the centre of the city, so we could go sightseeing if we wanted to, and treated us like royalty. I learnt such a lot about arterial surgery, and of course Simon was the perfect companion." She hadn't noticed Simon and David arrive and stand in the doorway of the office, listening to every word, as she carried on speaking. Katrina clenched her fists as her sister spoke gaily. "He took me out to dinner every night, and we got on so well together. We're going out for dinner together as soon as he gets back into the country. He's coming home tomorrow, so I'm going to the airport to pick him up. He's a very special person you know, and I think he's falling for me, and of course I

could really fall for him."
"Funny, my memories of the Amsterdam trip are completely different to that" Simon spoke dryly from the doorway. "I don't remember taking you out for dinner at all, I certainly have no intention of taking you out for dinner tomorrow, and I definitely haven't fallen for you." Katrina had swung round at the sound of his voice, and swayed, as she did so. She had been feeling light headed all day, knowing that she should have eaten something, but there hadn't been time to spare. "Simon!" Eleanor said, with a smile, "I was just joking with Katy." Simon left the doorway and entered the office. "It didn't sound like a joke" he said, then he saw Katrina's pallor. "Katy?" he said, then "Katy" he said again urgently and held out a hand, but she could feel her head spinning, then everything went black, and she collapsed in a heap on the floor. David had sprung forward, and was assisting Simon as the two men looked after his sibling. "Go and get a trolley to put her on" he ordered his sister, and Eleanor, scared at the way Katrina had fallen, went to do her brothers orders. Simon was feeling for a pulse, and now he looked carefully at Katy's face. "What the hell has she been up to?" he muttered, raising an eyelid to look at her pupil reactions, but David was listening to her heart with a stethoscope he had produced from his pocket. "I don't think there's anything much wrong with her. I think she's just exhausted. Look at the dark marks under her eyes. She's very dehydrated as well." Eleanor had bought a trolley forward, and Simon lifted her. "Hell, she's lost so much weight" he said, as he picked her up to place her on it. The

commotion had bought other people into the corridor and Darren James had come to the door of the theatre. "What the hell is the problem?" he demanded. "Can't you keep the noise down?" and Bella, who had run to see how Katrina was, turned to look at him. "As it's your fault Katrina's so exhausted, I don't think you've got any right to demand that we keep the noise down. You've done nothing but demean her, and make her stay late to finish your lists, when everybody has told you there aren't enough staff."

"Leave it Bella" Simon said quietly, "We'll go into the reasons in a while. Meantime, Dave and I will take Katy down to A&E and see what's wrong with her." he turned to Eleanor who was standing frozen by the door. "You stay here and wait for us, and don't even think about sending for another patient, even if Darren insists." he ordered coldly. "Bella, stay here with Eleanor, and I'll let you know how Katy is when we find out ourselves." and he started to push the trolley out of the department. David went with him, and they were soon being attended to in the A&E department. The staff nurse in charge, called the consultant in the department to come and see to Katy, knowing that she was a senior member of staff, and had a consultant to accompany her. Simon had wrapped the blood pressure cuff round Katy's upper arm, and was looking at the machine, frowning, as he read the numbers. He looked up and saw the consultant come in. "Hi Ian, David, this is Ian Kerr, he's one of the consultants in this department. Ian, this is David Howarth" he introduced David to the consultant, who was a friend of his. "He's Katrina's

brother, and he's a consultant at White Bay." The consultant smiled at them both, as he assessed Katrina. "We've already met, thanks. But I didn't know Sister Howarth was related to you? You never told me that." he looked at David, enquiringly.
"She's not the only one" David said with a smile. "Eleanor Howard is Katrina's twin sister. She changed her name, when she and I were both working at St. Anselm's, because it was so confusing. But Ian, what do you think is wrong with Katrina? Her BP is extremely low, her pulse is weak, she's dehydrated plus, and she looks exhausted." Simon, was holding Katrina's hand, feeling her pulse and looking very concerned. "My registrar told me she said she wasn't sleeping properly" he said. Katrina was examined intensively, but the consultant could find nothing wrong with her. "I think she's just completely exhausted." he said. "We'll admit her, and let her sleep it out" he said now. "I'll put a drip up on her, get some fluid back into her, hopefully that will get her BP up again, and we'll see how she is when she wakes up."
"Thanks Ian," Simon said, and didn't say anything when he saw David smile at the other consultant. "I'll come and sit with her, when I've sorted a few things out in theatre. Can you let me know which ward she'll be going to?" he asked, and Ian nodded. "I'll stay with her, until she wakes." Simon continued. David looked at his friend. "I'll stay with you." he murmured. "But let's get back to theatre, to find out what's happening" he smiled at the A&E consultant as he turned to leave. "Thanks Ian. I'll be back to see you later." Simon had noticed the friendship

between the two men, but said nothing, and they were walking out of the department as David spoke to Simon again. "Is that correct, that Darren James expects her to stay and work late, when they don't have enough staff?" Simon nodded. "I know she feels she has to stay because she's in charge of the department, but I don't know how much overtime she's done recently. When I talked to her before I had to go to the conference, she told me she'd done thirteen days without a day off. That's why I took her away for a weekend, just to make sure she got away from the unit, and I wouldn't have allowed her to go into work, if there had been a need." David whistled. "She can't go on like that" he said. The two men walked back to the theatre unit, and found Eleanor and Bella still in the office, waiting for them. "How is she?" Eleanor asked immediately, and Simon answered his house officer. "She's exhausted and very dehydrated, her blood pressure is so low it's amazing she was still upright, and she's now asleep. She'll have some more tests done, obviously, but hopefully, she'll be a lot better when she wakes up."

"Oh, thank goodness." Bella said. "But I've found out why she's so tired. I've just looked at the off-duty book, she hasn't had a day off for 19 days and she's done about 50- or 60-hours overtime since the start of the month." David was appalled at Bella's words, "How much?" he demanded. "That's nearly two weeks of overtime! Why the hell is she working such long hours?"

"Because we simply don't have enough staff. We're meant to have at least 22 trained staff and six students, but we're down to 14, and we don't have any students any more. And that's Darren James doing. He told the nursing officers that we aren't able to train them, so they don't come to us anymore." Bella said simply. "He won't let anybody else be appointed, he said we've got to work harder and we can do more overtime. Because Katrina is the senior, and the rest of us are also doing a lot of overtime, she's staying later and later, in order to finish his lists. He put five laparotomies on one list, a few weeks ago, plus an appendix, and despite what she said to him, he wouldn't cancel anything. She managed to get one of the Ortho staff to come up and finish his list on that day, but since then he's got even worse, and while you were away, she had to stay until 7.30 on two evenings, and 8.00 on the other two days when he had a list. And the following week was similar. He'd taken over your lists, Mr. Parker, because he wanted to make maximum use of them, and as you were away, he decided he'd use them. She never gets off duty before six or half past each evening, has had to scrap her half days, and doesn't always have a lunch break, and I can't remember the last time I saw her having a coffee break." David shook his head, and his face became set. "Where is Darren James?" he demanded, and on being told that he was still operating in theatre Three, but stitching up, he strode to the door, and flung it open. "I need to talk to you" he said to the surgeon at the table. "Leave the stitching up to your registrar, and come and talk to me in Sister's office, and under no circumstances is the next patient to be sent for." and he walked away, and back into the office. They two men only had a short wait, before Darren James appeared in the doorway, and David bared his teeth at him in a faux smile. "Good afternoon. Please come in and have a seat. I'd like to talk to you." he said, and Simon shut the door firmly behind the consultant, and stood leaning against it. David spoke, as Darren sat down. "I'm a consultant physician at White Bay Hospital. I've just been looking at the overtime book" he said. "Perhaps you'd like to have a look at it" and he pushed the book towards him. "This is the overtime record for Sister Howarth" he said, as he pointed to the figures. "As you can see, she's done a very large amount of overtime just recently. At least fifty hours in fact, and probably more. And most of it appears to be for your operating lists. And these are the records for the rest of the girls. They are also having to do large amounts of overtime. What do you have to say about that?"

"Nothing" blustered the consultant surgeon. "She obviously doesn't manage her staff properly, doesn't put enough people on in the evenings, so she has to stay late herself."

"She doesn't have enough staff to put them on in the evenings" David said angrily, "For this department, the minimum number of staff needed is twenty-two trained staff. Sister Howarth has fourteen, barely enough to cover. I understand you won't allow Miss Betts, the nursing officer, to appoint any more staff, and this theatre isn't the only one that is suffering. What do you have to say to that?"

"I don't know who the hell you are?" Darren James snorted, but David didn't introduce himself. "I told you, I'm an independent consultant from White Bay hospital" he said. "I've been bought in, because the senior medical and nursing staff here are so worried about the health of their companions, and they couldn't get an appointment to see the committee, because they weren't going to meet for a while, and that, I understand, is also down to you. The overtime book shows that every member of staff has at least thirty hours of overtime owing to them, just for this month alone, and I also understand that they don't get paid for it."

"No, they have to take the time back in lieu" Darren James said, but now Simon spoke at the same time as Bella. "When?" he demanded.

"When the hell do we get the opportunity to take time back? We work all the hours God sends as it is." Bella demanded, but Simon shushed her. "Hang on Bella" he said quietly, and the other girl subsided, and David continued. "I understand you are on the committee, and you persuaded your companions, that staff shouldn't be appointed and the girls shouldn't be paid overtime," he said quietly, and Darren James nodded. "There isn't enough money for them to be paid" he said but David laughed mirthlessly. "On the contrary, I have been informed that there was enough money to appoint fifteen more medical staff in the past two months alone. For the same amount of money, at least twenty or thirty nurses could have been appointed, and this situation wouldn't have arisen. I know it's a different budget" he said, before Darren James could interrupt, "but in circumstances like this, the budgets can be altered, and the money used for nurses instead. Maybe your colleagues on the committee would like to come and spend a few days in theatre and see how much work the girls actually do undertake. And it's not only these theatres that are understaffed. Every single one has problems with staff numbers. They don't have student nurses coming to assist either, and I understand that it was you who stopped them coming to work in theatre."

"Yes." Darren James said nonchalantly. "My daughter is a student nurse, and she told me that they weren't being trained properly when they came to theatres, so I told the nursing officers that it wasn't right to send them here." David sat back in his chair and watched, then before the other man could say anything, he leant forward again. "We will discuss that later on, but Sister Howarth will now be off sick for at least three weeks. You saw that she collapsed this evening?" he queried, and Darren James nodded. "I expect she was putting it on" he said, and David had to hold Simon back, as the other man tried to get nearer to the other consultant. "On the contrary" he said quietly, "she collapsed because she is completely exhausted, which was caused through overwork," David said, "and in order to be able to recover properly, she needs the time off. I will not allow the other girls to take her duties onto their shoulders, so there will have to be a radical rethink about the amount of work to be put onto the operating lists, which I will be doing, and cancelling cases when I feel it is necessary."

"You can't do that" Darren James said angrily, and stared angrily as Simon laughed at him. "On the contrary, I can. I have been given those powers by the theatre superintendent." David said quietly. "Now, I suggest you go and cancel the rest of your list, and feed the patients, because there will not be any more operating tonight." he turned to Eleanor, "Dr. Howard, please go with Mr. James and make sure that the patients still waiting for surgery are fed. The only operating that will be done tonight is the emergency list." Without a word, Eleanor followed the surgeon out of the room, and there was silence until she came back into the room, and sat down in front of her brother. "Okay Elly," he said quietly "I want to know what's been happening here." David said, "I understand you've been pushing your sister to stay late on quite a few occasions as well. Anything to say about that?"

"It was a bit of a joke really" she said quietly. "I wanted to impress the other surgeons. I didn't mean to make Katy ill, honest."

"You saw how ill she looked this afternoon, yet you were still trying to get her to stay. Don't say anything now, but we will talk some other time. Are you off duty now?" Eleanor nodded "Yes, as Darren's list has been stopped, I'm free from now on, but I'm on call tomorrow night and over the weekend" she said, and David looked at her. "Okay, go home now, don't talk about this to anybody, but you'd better be aware that I'm not happy about the whole situation. I will talk to you tomorrow, when I've done a bit more investigating, so make sure you will be available. Get Ewan Dexter's SHO to cover for you, while we talk."

"Can I go and sit with Katy until she wakes up?" she asked, but David shook his head. "No, I don't think so." he said. "I don't think she'd want to see you at the moment, even if she is awake. No Elly, just leave Katy alone for the moment." Eleanor smiled at her brother, but he didn't smile back. "I'm sorry Dave." she said again, before she went to get changed. Bella was left with Simon and David. "Are you really Katrina's brother?" she asked him, and when he nodded, she smiled. "She told me that she had a brother, who is a consultant at White Bay. How on earth did you think about telling David James that you were an independent consultant bought in to look at the situation?" she asked, and he smiled at her. "Because I was" he said simply. "Anne Betts and Ian Davidson were so worried about the problems, and decided that something needed to be done, so they asked me if I'd come and have a look at the situation, because they haven't been able to get an appointment with the committee to try and make them understand what's been happening. I've been given carte blanche by the entire theatre management team to try and sort things out, which is why I could order Darren James to cancel the rest of his list." He grinned at the other girl, then asked, "Who is on a late duty tonight?" Bella smiled at him. "As it happens, I'm the senior tonight. If we can just get on with the emergency list, then things will be easier. Thanks for your help." and she left the room. David and Simon exchanged glances, then got to their feet, made sure that everything else was okay in the department, and went back to A&E to be with Katy, before a bed was found for her in a ward.

Chapter Seven

When Katrina opened her eyes in the early hours of the next morning, she became aware that her brother was sitting by her bedside. “I had a dream about you” she mumbled, then turned on her side, and was asleep again. David sat back and watched her. She had been totally exhausted, he thought, and wondered again how a surgeon such as Darren James, who took such good care of his patients, had allowed her and the rest of the nursing staff, to work such long hours without a break. He looked up, as Simon came back into the side room, where they had been sitting with Katrina. “She woke up, mumbled that she'd had a dream about me, and went straight back to sleep again. Why not go home Simon? She's in good hands here, and I don't think she'll wake up again very soon.” His friend shook his head. “No, I'll stay.” he said. “If you want to, you could crash at my place, and come back in the morning. Or is it urgent that you get back to White Bay?”

“No, because I've been asked to give my opinion about the running of the theatres here, the hospital have agreed to let me have some time away, and my patients are being seen by my colleagues. I can stay for a few days. But I think it might be an idea to get some sleep. I can go and sleep at Ian’s place for a few hours, then I can come back and relieve you for a sleep later on.” He obviously hadn't realised how much information he had given the other man, and Simon didn't say anything. “Thanks” Simon said as David left, and he was left alone with Katrina, and he reached out to take her hand in his. He and David had been to her flat, to collect some nightwear and toiletries for her, and he had found one of the postcards he had sent her, under her pillow, but couldn't understand why she had only kept that one. He had sent her one each day, as well as a few long letters, but there had been no sign of those. Katrina stirred, and she turned onto her back, the drip going into her arm, moving as she did so. He carefully adjusted its position, and sat back down by her side. He was holding her hand again, as the night staff nurse on duty came into the room, took her observations before charting them, and he smiled at her. "How's her pressure?" he asked, and the nurse held out the chart for him to see. Thankfully her blood pressure had risen, and he was glad that it had. "Do you want a cup of tea?" the nurse asked, and he thanked her and accepted. The staff on the ward had been extremely helpful, knowing as they did, that there were two consultants keeping an eye on her, and Katrina was a sister in theatre herself. She bought him the tea on a tray, and checked Katrina's drip, before she turned to face him. "What the hell happened to her?" she asked him, her voice quiet in the darkened room. "We don't have much to do with the theatre nurses, being a medical ward, but some of us know Katrina, and we wondered how she managed to get into this state? She's lost so much weight, and she looks so ill. I understand she collapsed in theatres yesterday, but I can't understand how nobody saw how ill she was before that."

"It's a long story Staff, but she's been working too hard, because there aren't enough staff, she's being

doing too much overtime, and nobody was able to do anything. I returned from a study trip yesterday, and was there just in time to see her collapse." Simon said quietly, "But let me ask you something. Are you short of nursing staff on the wards? There's been a problem in theatres, but I don't know about the wards. Are they in a similar state?"
"Well, they were" she answered him. "The committee didn't want too many nurses to be appointed, but our managers managed to persuade them, that we just didn't have enough nursing staff to cope, and told them they'd have to close a ward, purely and simply because there weren't enough nurses to staff it." Simon nodded. "I thought it might have been something like that" he said. "Don't worry about Katrina. I'll look after her, if you're busy."
"Thanks" she said. "We are a bit rushed tonight. But just ring if you need me for anything." and she went back into the main ward again. Simon went back to the bedside and taking Katrina's hand again, he settled down to wait.

Katrina was asleep for nearly three complete days, only opening her eyes on a couple of occasions, but never when Simon was by her side, and it was the early evening of the third day, when he had taken up his station by the bed again, when she started to rouse. He immediately put down the papers he had been working on, and waited for her to open her eyes. She stretched, then opened her eyes properly, and saw him. "Hello" she said, then closed her eyes again, before opening them again. "Where am I?"

she asked, as she registered the fact that she was in a room that wasn't hers. "You're in the side room of Donaldson ward" he said, matter of factly, and she frowned. "Why? And why have I got a drip up?" she asked "what happened?"

"Do you remember talking to Elly about Amsterdam?" he asked, and she frowned, as she tried to remember, then the memories came flooding back. "Yes" she said eventually, "then you came into the office with David, and I can't remember anything after that."

"No," he smiled at her. "You've been asleep ever since then. Your parents are coming back in this evening to see how you are, David is working around the hospital talking to various people, and keeps on coming to check up on you, and Eleanor is very worried about you and has rung up very frequently to see how you are."

"Why the hell are my parents coming to see me?" she wanted to know. "I've only had a sleep. I presume I fainted, so why am I in a hospital bed, and why the drip?"

"You collapsed in the office, just after David and I entered it. Your blood pressure was so low it was almost unreadable, and you were totally exhausted. Ian Kerr, the A&E consultant decided that you should be admitted, and you've been here since Wednesday evening." Katrina struggled to sit up in the bed, and stared at him. "I only fainted" she complained. "I can't understand why I was admitted."

"Because it's now Saturday afternoon. You've been asleep for nearly three days." he told her, and she looked at him with shock. "Three days!" she exclaimed. "I knew I was tired, but that's ridiculous." He smiled at her. "You were totally exhausted" he said. "We've all seen the overtime book. You hadn't had a day off for 19 days, you'd worked over 50 hours overtime in the month, in addition to your normal working days, and it was only a question of time before your body decided that you needed a rest, and shut itself down so you could get one."

"The department needed to be covered" she excused herself. "I had to cover for Bella one weekend, because she was unwell, and the following weekend, there was a multiple pile up on the motorway, and we all got called in for hours at a time. Darren James wouldn't cancel any patients, and his lists went on and on, and we didn't have enough staff, so somebody had to stay and scrub for them, and while you were away, he started using your lists to do more of his cases."

"Your brother was asked by Miss Betts and Ian Davidson, to come and have a poke around to find out why everybody was working so hard." he grinned as he spoke, "In actual fact, they asked for a consultant to come, and he offered. I don't know whether they knew beforehand, that he is your sibling, but believe me, he's doing his level best to make sure that everybody on the committee realises what has been happening in the theatres. But it explains why you never answered your phone when I tried to contact you from Amsterdam. You were never in the flat, you were obviously working."

"Why didn't you try my mobile?" she asked, but he shook his head. "If you'd charged it up, I would have been able to do that, but when we found it in your

locker, it's completely dead. You can't have charged it up for a very long time." She nodded, "I don't think I've had time to charge it up." she said. "But to be completely honest. I didn't think about it,"
"Obviously" he said. "I'm going to let the nurse know that you're awake, and then we can get you something to eat. When was the last time you had a meal? You haven't been eating again, have you?"
"I had a meal with Joe and Sarah on Monday evening." she argued, but he shook his head. "And I bet you haven't had a proper meal since then, have you?" She gave in, and agreed with him, and watched as he left the side room. The nurse came in then, took her observations, made sure she was doing alright, and asked her what she fancied to eat.
"This is going to sound really awful, but I really fancy fish and chips – nice crisp batter and lashings of salt and vinegar, and a pot of tea" she replied with a smile, "but I don't think I'm going to get that, am I? But anything will do, thanks."
"We'll see" she said with a smile. "Your mum and dad are here, and waiting to see you. I'll tell them you're ready, shall I?" Katrina nodded and a minute later, her parents came in to see her. "Oh, thank goodness you're awake" her mother said, as she gave her a big hug. "I was so worried about you, when David told us what had happened." Her father joined his wife at her bedside, and started to talk to her, asking her how she felt, telling her news of the family. "I can't believe how exhausted you obviously were" her father said after they had talked for a while. "I can't understand it." he said, "I would never have let any of the nurses who I worked with,

work themselves silly like you've been doing. I can't understand why that James man wouldn't let the committee appoint more nurses. I've been talking to the ward staff, and they were having the same problems, but the committee appointed more staff for them, so why not the theatres as well?"
"Because he's a nasty piece of work" David said from the doorway. "I've been talking to some of the other members of the committee, and a lot of the other surgical consultant staff who he had been talking to, and he basically told them that theatres didn't need more staff, there were enough to go around, it just needed somebody to do the rotas properly. I think he was trying to force their hands to try and get rid of you, Katy."
"Well, he's never liked me, and didn't want me to be appointed in the first place" she admitted, as David came and gave her a big hug. "I've stood up to him on more than one occasion about the length of his lists, but I didn't realise he was trying to get rid of me." She grinned at him. "I'm sorry if I gave you a shock, collapsing in front of you."
"It was quite dramatic, but I think Simon was more shocked and worried about you" he said, "he certainly hasn't left your side for more than a couple of hours at a time, since you were admitted."
"You're joking!" she exclaimed, "Why has he stayed here?"
"Oh Katy" said her mother, "if you don't know now, you soon will do. He'll be back in a few minutes, and he can tell you himself." She and her father prepared to leave. "We'll go now, and let you get some rest, as you still look tired, but we'll be back tomorrow"

she said. "I don't think you'll be discharged until Monday at the earliest, so we'll see you tomorrow," and she bent and kissed her daughter. They left the room, followed by David after saying their farewells, and Katrina was left on her own for a short while, to think about things that had been said, but then the door opened, and Simon came in, bearing a parcel, which she could smell, contained fish and chips. He grinned at her as he said, "You told the nurse you fancied this, and as I think you deserve a treat, and the nurse didn't object, I went and got some for you." He arranged everything on her bed table, and sat down to watch her eat the food and poured out the tea the nurse bought in for her. When everything had been eaten, Katrina gathered the wrappers together, and sat back against the pillows, and Simon had come to sit on the edge of the bed, and pushed the bed table away. "That was absolutely lovely" she said. "I think I'd been dreaming about a meal like that. But have you had anything to eat? David said you'd been here all the time I was asleep. That must have been really boring, just watching me sleep and probably snoring my head off."

"You weren't snoring" he said quietly, "and I've had plenty to eat, and I was able to catch up on the paperwork. But I wouldn't leave you until you were awake."

"Why?" she asked him quietly, and he took her hand in his. "Do you really have to ask?" he said. "Katy, my darling Katy, I love you so much, I would do anything for you, and to see you so white and looking so ill, tore my heart out. I didn't want to have to leave you to go to Amsterdam, and I made up my mind that as soon as I got back, I was going to ask you to marry me. But then I was asked to go to Utrecht to do one of my big arterial operations, and I couldn't refuse, so I was extremely glad when the patient recovered so quickly, and I was able to get back a day early. I bumped into David at the airport, he suggested I spent the night at his house, before he bought me back here the following day, and we came to the theatres to surprise you. But I was the one who got the surprise, you looked at me when I came into the office, then you collapsed. I couldn't stop worrying about you, I certainly wouldn't have been able to work properly, so Joe has been doing the smaller cases, and I just stayed here with you, and I've been catching up on some paperwork, while I waited for you to wake. But now I can ask you. Katy, my beloved, darling Katy, will you marry me?" He was holding her hand tight, and she nodded. "Yes," she said, "yes, I will. I've loved you for a long time" she didn't get a chance to complete her sentence, for she was in Simon's arms, and he was kissing her, as if his heart would break if he didn't. They didn't hear the nurse open the door, look in, and then close the door quietly behind her, but as she went into the main ward again, she was smiling broadly.

When they eventually broke the kiss, and she was able to think clearly again, Katrina reached out to touch his face. "Oh Simon" she said "I've missed you so much. But you didn't phone me, while you were away, and I couldn't get in touch with you, because the phone went straight to voicemail when I tried to

phone you. No, you phoned me twice, when you first got there" she said, trying to be fair. Simon shook his head. "No, I phoned you every night, as I said, you obviously weren't in, you were working hard, and I wasn't there to stop you. I tried several times each evening, before our meal, but I had to go to meetings in the evenings, but they always ran late, and I wasn't going to phone you at midnight, and risk waking you up."
"But I got your postcard" she said. "I loved that, and thank you for writing it."
"I wrote to you every day" he told her. "I made sure that I sent you at least a postcard every day, and I wrote you letters as well."
"I only received one postcard" she said softly. "Maybe the post wasn't brilliant so I didn't get them." He kissed her again, "well, I'm here now" he said, "and we'll get married very soon, and I'll be able to make sure you don't try and kill yourself with overwork again." She yawned, and he gently let her go. "I think you need some more rest" he said, "I'll let you go back to sleep, and I'll be here tomorrow morning. I'll talk to your consultant tomorrow and see if I can take you home on Monday afternoon. Your parents are staying at your flat tonight, but I imagine they'll be going home tomorrow, now that they know you're alright. Goodnight my darling girl." He kissed her gently on the lips, she smiled at him, and lay back, closed her eyes and was soon asleep. Simon watched for a moment, then bent his head, kissed her on the forehead and softly left the room.

The following afternoon, as she had recovered,

and her bed was needed urgently for an emergency case, she was allowed to be discharged into his care, and David took her to Simon's house, so that she would not be seen leaving the hospital with Simon. She had asked the ward nurse to say nothing about what had been seen the night before, and as she had known Katrina a long time, she had agreed. Katrina had been to Simon's house on several occasions, and liked it very much and as he opened the front door to admit her, she felt as though she had come home. David wouldn't stay, saying he would be in touch, and soon left them alone, so she was curled up in the corner of the settee, when Simon bought her a cup of tea, and she looked up and smiled at him. "Thank you" she said "I'm going to miss this attention when I go back to work tomorrow."

"You're not going back tomorrow" he said firmly. "You need time off to recover from the work you've been doing, and your brother has pulled a few strings, and you're going to have three weeks off sick." She sat up straight and stared at him. "He didn't tell me that. I can't have three weeks off" she stated. "We don't have enough staff for me to take that amount of time off. The other girls will have to cover for me, and they're busy enough as it is. I don't want to risk them getting ill as well."

"It's all sorted," he said soothingly, "White Bay's theatres were going to be out of action for a while, because they've got to have something done to the roof, so their girls were going to be lent out to the wards, but David has arranged for some of them to come over and help out. There are more than enough staff to cover the fact that you're not there.

Plus, Darren James won't be working, he has been suspended because of what he's been doing to you and the rest of the staff, and the rest of the lists won't be enormous. Your brother ordered an immediate meeting of the committee, and told them exactly what had been happening. They really didn't know what exactly what was going on, because Darren James had lied and told them that you were coping well, and the reports from Ian Davidson weren't being passed on, because Darren was keeping them. They were all disgusted, and they decided to suspend him for a while. He's also been removed from the committee, so he won't be able to try and interfere in future. His registrar will be doing his lists, and he won't be doing any very big cases. The other surgeons have been talked to, and they've agreed that they will cut down the number of cases they do each week, until you get some more staff. They didn't realise exactly how bad the staffing situation actually was, because of what Darren James had told them. Miss Betts will phone you tomorrow, and she'll tell you how the situation is going to resolve itself, but you're going to get more staff, that's a promise. And the students will be coming back as well. The fact that you actually collapsed through overwork made everybody realise how hard all you girls have been working." He grinned at her, "so I'll be able to come home, and find you here waiting for me, when I've finished a day's work, and treat you like a princess." He pulled her into his arms, and held her close to kiss her. "Enjoy your time off my darling." She gave in then, and kissed him back, and for a while there was silence in the room, as they pleasured each other. When at last he drew back, he grinned at her. "Your tea is going to be cold" he said. "I'll go and make you another one in a minute." but she shook her head. "Don't bother" she said with a smile. "I think I like your alternative to a cup of tea." He grinned at her, and took her into his arms again, to kiss and caress her, and make her feel wanted.

Later that evening, as she cuddled close to him, as they sat together, he asked her about the wedding. "Do you want a big wedding, that takes six months to organise, and costs a fortune, or do you want a quiet ceremony? I know which one I'd prefer, but it's your choice my darling."
"Just a very small wedding, with just us and our families." she answered. "And the sooner the better, as far as I'm concerned." He kissed her gently. "I'm so glad you said that" he said. "I can get some leave in about a week's time, and you'll still be off sick, so shall I get a special licence and we can have the ceremony as soon as I can arrange it?" She nodded and reached up to kiss him. "It sounds so good to me." she said. "I can't wait to be your wife." He kissed her and there was no more talk.

When he arrived home on the Tuesday evening, he was grinning widely as he took her into his arms and greeted her. "Your staff have been told that you've been discharged, and everybody wants to know how you are. David has told them that you're recovering with your parents, but won't give the phone number so they can phone you. But it's obvious that nobody in Donaldson ward, told the rest of the staff that I've been with you, because your staff haven't worked out yet, that we're a couple." Katy nodded. "I asked the girls there, not to say a word" she said. "I wanted to keep everything a secret before we announce it." He grinned, kissed her, then continued "But the atmosphere in theatres is so very different to what it was. There are enough staff and to spare, the fact that Darren James isn't there is making everybody very happy, and of course, all the lists have been cut down ruthlessly. David is keeping an eagle eye on things that are happening there, and Miss Betts came in this morning and sent Bella and Anne off for a few days, to take some of their time back, and Janet is in charge. She's going to leave tomorrow, and that way she'll get her time back. She's got your mobile number so she's going to phone you tonight to say goodbye. Miss Betts said she was going to phone you. Did she?" Katrina nodded, "She wanted to know exactly how I was, made sure that I won't be back before my sick leave is up, told me not to worry about anything, and then told me off for doing too much overtime." she grinned. "I don't think she meant it, but she told me not to do anything like that, ever again." Simon grinned at her. "I will make sure you don't" he said, as he kissed her. She had made him a coffee, which she handed to him, and he grinned. "I'll definitely drink this." and they smiled at each other. It was as they sat together, drinking their coffee, that he frowned, and said, "I'm quite worried about Eleanor" he said. "She didn't come into theatre on Monday, and I haven't really had time to talk to her, but she

was so subdued today, didn't laugh or smile at anything, didn't want to do too much during the surgery, and was very efficient. Totally different to how she normally behaves."
"Did she come and see me when I was in hospital?" Katrina asked, but he thought for a while, then shook his head. "She phoned several times, and I was able to reassure her, that you were okay, still sleeping, but she was on call and she was quite busy, Joe said."
"Did you let her know that I was home?" and he nodded. "David told her you were staying with your parents, and you were fine. He had told her that you'd been given some sick leave, and he said she seemed fine about it. Maybe she's sickening for something"
"When we can set the date, I'll phone her and tell her that we're getting married. But I think I'll phone her tonight and see if she's okay. Despite what she tried to do to me, she is still my twin sister, and I don't want her to be too upset." Simon kissed her gently. "She will be a good doctor when she settles down a bit. I'm sorry you weren't able to do your medical degree, but if you had, I'd probably never have met you, so there is a bright spot to it." He kissed her again, then leant forward and picked up his cup. "I told you, I'm definitely drinking this" he said, and grinned as he drank it down, then put the cup down, and took her in his arms again, and kissed her long and hard. She didn't care about the dinner she was cooking, just wanted to be with him, and knew that she loved him more with each passing day. Eventually he lifted his head, and she got her breath

back. “If the dinner is burnt, it’s your fault” she said with a smile, and reluctantly got off the settee, to go out to the kitchen. He followed her out, and allowed her to check her cooking, before he gave her a hug, and kissed the back of her neck. “I love you” he whispered, “and you've got no idea how much I longed to be able to do this to you while I was away.” She turned to face him, reached up and kissed him. “I didn't know if you wanted to continue seeing me when you got back from the conference” she said. “I fell in love with you, when you took me out for dinner the second time. I didn't want to, but I'm glad I did. Before you took me out for a drink, we seemed to rub each other up the wrong way, and after that evening, things seemed to be better between us. Then we went for dinner, and I knew that I did like you, but it was when we went out the second time, and you kissed me, I knew I loved you. I didn't want to love you, but I'm glad I do.” He kissed her again, “I fell in love with you the very first time I saw you when I started here” he said. “You didn't seem to get on with me, and when we did that appendix that turned out to be an aneurysm after the main list that went on for ages, I didn't think I would stand a chance at getting you to love me. I didn't know how to change your mind. I'm very pleased that you did.” He kissed her gently, they smiled at each other, then he let her go to finish cooking the dinner.

They had eaten and were sitting together on the settee, when the phone rang. Simon answered it, and listened intently to the person on the other end.

"Okay" he said eventually, "I'll come in. I'll be with you in about 10 minutes." He put the phone down, and gently kissed Katrina. "I've got to go in" he said. "I don't think I'll be too late, but I'll be back when I can. Go to bed, if I'm not back. You still need your sleep and I think you should continue to have early nights, while you're recovering." He kissed her again, before he grinned at her, and she knew what his suggestion of an early night entailed. "Why don't you phone Eleanor and have a chat with her, and see what's wrong with her. She sounded very weird today. Have a talk with her, and see if you can find out what's troubling her." She nodded, kissed him and urged him to go. "The sooner you go, the sooner you'll be back. Drive safely won't you. I'll see you soon." He kissed her again, and reluctantly left the house.

Left alone, Katrina decided to see what was bothering her sister. She couldn't remember ever hearing that Eleanor was so subdued, and decided to talk to her. When her sister answered, Katrina was quick to tell her that she was a lot better than she had been, and was taking some time off on sick leave. "David arranged it all" she said. "I've been told to take three weeks off, so I'll be able to catch up on my sleep. I woke up late this morning, and I'm going to bed early this evening, so I'll soon be back to my normal self." Eleanor didn't say anything, and Katrina frowned. "What's the matter Elly?" she said gently, "I've been told that you were very subdued at work today, and didn't laugh or joke with anybody. What's the problem?" and she was perturbed, when her sister burst into tears. Katrina didn't know what to say, but Eleanor kept on repeating, "I'm sorry Katy, I'm so sorry." When her sister's sobs subsided, Katy said firmly, "come on Elly, what's the problem, and why do you feel you need to apologise to me? Or is it that you think you're responsible for me collapsing? That you'd pushed me into doing too much work? What is it."

"I can't explain Katy, but I'm so sorry." Eleanor repeated. "I've done some stupid things in my time, and I've hurt you, and I didn't want to. It started out as a joke, but things went too quick for me to stop them. Oh Katy, I'm so sorry" she repeated, and put the phone down. Katrina tried to contact her sister several times, but Eleanor didn't answer, and eventually, Katrina went to bed, knowing that Simon was going to be kept at the hospital for quite a while, and wanting to talk to him, but unable to do so. She thought she was too wide awake to sleep, but she was still tired, and slid over the edge into a refreshing sleep. When Simon came home later that night, she was curled up in bed, deeply asleep, and he smiled at the sight. She was infinitely precious to him, and he was so glad they were to be married. Their relationship was still a secret, and he was glad, for he wanted nothing to be said that could hurt her. When he and David had seen her collapse the previous week, he had felt helpless, and unable to give her any assistance at all, and he had been so glad when she had woken up, and he had been able to tell her how he felt. He knew he had been remiss in not telling her sooner how he felt about her, had never told her before that he loved her, but he thought she might have realised that. In the light of the street lamp coming through the curtains, he could see the shape of the box that was on his dressing table. He still hadn't shown her what he had bought for her in Amsterdam, and hoped she would like it. He had been wandering around the jewellery quarter in the town, when he had seen the engagement ring he had bought for her. It was a large emerald, surrounded by diamonds, and with smaller emeralds set between the white stones, and he had envisaged it on Katy's finger, and had bought it, there and then. As he slid between the sheets, and cuddled her close, he smiled, as he closed his eyes and slept dreamlessly, until the alarm woke him in the morning.

Chapter Eight

Katrina had recovered very well, and although she was still very thin, she was gaining weight slowly, and sleeping well. At the end of her first week of sick leave, Simon had taken her out for a meal one evening, and they were sitting in the restaurant he had chosen, when he presented her with the ring he had bought. "I wanted to give you this when I asked you to marry me" he said, as she gazed in awe at the gems. "But you were just recovering from your collapse, and I wasn't going to do so then, as you were about to fall asleep on me again. And since then, I've wanted to give it to you, but I've been busy, or I've been prevented from giving it to you. I'm sorry Katy. Does it suit you, or would you like something different?"

"Oh Simon, it's beautiful, and I'd love to wear it. Will you put it on for me please?" and she held out her hand. Simon took the ring, and pushed it onto her finger, then picked up her hand and kissed it. "That was a good guess, about the size of your finger" he said gruffly, but Katrina wasn't fooled, and knew he was hiding strong emotion. She took his hand in hers, and held it tight. "I love you so much" she whispered. "And I love you" he replied, and smiled and looked at her with love in his eyes. They were enjoying their meal, when Simon drew her attention to the other side of the room. "Have you seen who's over there in the corner?" he asked, and she turned her head, to see her brother sitting with another man, who reached out to touch his hand, and then keep hold of it. They were smiling at each other and they both looked very happy, and she smiled at the sight. "Do you know him?" she asked and he nodded. "That's Ian Kerr, he's one of the consultants in A&E, and he's the guy who admitted you after your collapse." He laughed, then continued, "and to think I introduced David to him when we took you down to A&E. It's obvious they know each other very well already." She joined in his laughter, then said "I do hope he and David will be happy together. He looks a nice guy." Simon nodded. "We've known each other for quite a while, and he's always come across as very pleasant. Actually, David didn't realise but he told me he was going to stay at Ian's house when I told him to get some sleep, and I don't think he realised how much information he had given me." They became engrossed in their meal again, talking about their future and the plans for their wedding, and it was as they were leaving the restaurant, that David saw them, and beckoned them across, got to his feet and hugged her close. "You look a lot better than you did when I took you back to Simon's house when you were discharged." he told his sister, then saw the engagement ring on her finger. "Well, it's taken long enough" he said, "but I'm glad you've made up your minds. When is the wedding going to be?" Simon and Katrina exchanged glances. "Very soon" Simon said. "You'll get an invitation."

"Oh good" said David, then remembered his manners. "Of course, Simon, you two know each other already, but Katy, this is Ian" he introduced his companion, "he's a friend of mine" and Katrina laughed, knowing what he was implying. "We haven't been introduced until now, but we have met,

I believe" she said, and Ian smiled as he stood, and kissed her cheek. "Indeed, we have. You look a lot better than you did the last time I saw you."
"I feel a lot better, thank you" she answered. "I don't remember much about that day – it had been hectic and I'd been scrubbed all day, I hadn't eaten or drunk anything, and I only stopped to draw breath and have a chat with my sister, before I went off duty, and I must have turned round too quickly and fainted."
"The sight of two consultants pushing a theatre trolley with a theatre sister on it, through the corridors must have been entertaining. But it's nice to finally meet you and be able to talk to you. David's told me a lot about you." Ian said with a smile, "And none of it was good, I expect" she said, but Ian shook his head, and smiled at David as he said, "All of it was very good. He said he's told you a lot of things he hasn't been able to tell other people." he said, and she nodded, knowing exactly what he meant. They chatted together for a while, before they said their goodbyes, and went on their way. "Poor David" she said as she got into the car. "It's going to be difficult for them both, until people start to accept them as a couple."
"Poor David, nothing" Simon said "he's well able to take any criticism, but I don't suppose that anybody will be too upset about it, and in any event, it's nobody's business, but theirs. There are plenty of gay couples around these days anyway, so they're not considered abnormal any more by anybody. I don't think anybody I know considers it wrong these days." Katrina agreed, and the talk turned to other

matters. “How's Eleanor's behaviour these days?” she asked him, and he shook his head. “She's still not acting as she used to. Even some of your staff have said that. They can't believe how different she is. Did she give you any indication of what the problem is?” Katrina shook her head. “No, she just kept on saying she was sorry, until she put the phone down on me. She won't answer me at all now. I think I'll go and see her tomorrow, and see how she is.”

“I'll come with you” he offered, but she shook her head. “No, I think it would be better if I went on my own. I'll tell her I've gone back to my own flat, and she can come and see me, or I can go into her room at the doctor’s house.” He kissed her hand gently, then concentrated on his driving again. “I've got one of my big arterial cases tomorrow” he muttered, as they drew up outside the house, “and I'll be on call in the evening, so I don't think I'll be home very early” he said, as they walked up the path to the front door. “But I should be able to get home before you go to bed.” He opened the door and they went in, and he closed the door behind them, before he pulled her into his arms, and kissed her deeply. “Do you want coffee?” she asked, but he grinned “No” he said gently, “I want you,” before he bent, picked her up, and carried her up the stairs to their bedroom, where he laid her on the bed, and came to lie down beside her to kiss her gently, then with more passion. Their love making was incredible, as it always was, and she knew she loved him more with every passing day.

The next day, she knew that Eleanor was on duty

in the hospital, and bleeped her, so that she would have no idea of who was phoning, to allow her sister to ignore her, and when Eleanor answered, she was eager to talk to her. "Elly, it's Katy." she said quickly, "Don't hang up please, Elly, I need to talk to you. You're not on call tonight, are you? Will you come and talk to me at the flat tonight? I'll cook you something to eat, and we can have a long talk about things." she stopped talking and wondered what her sister would say, then drew in a sigh of relief, as Eleanor said quietly. "Okay. What time do you want me to arrive?"

They made their arrangements, and when she put the phone down, Katrina knew that she would be able to have a talk with her sister, and hopefully find out what was bothering her.

The flat, when she reached it, was cold and had an un-lived in air about it, so she swiftly made a list, went shopping for food for that evening, and went back to dust the flat and get it ready for her sister's visit. Her parents, who had stayed there when she was in hospital, had changed the sheets before leaving, but put the sheets ready for washing, so she set the washing machine going, and rooted around the wardrobe, to find something else to wear. She settled on a blouse and skirt, and decided to continue wearing her engagement ring, and wondered if Elly would notice it and say anything and although she didn't want to keep secrets from her sister, she had decided not to mention it, until she could a spend a lot more time with her, and explain fully. She and Simon had talked to her parents, who were understandably delighted at their engagement, had agreed to keep everything secret, and had made arrangements for all the family to visit on a day at the end of the week, along with Simon's sisters, and they would then announce that they were all to see them married, and go to the church, where the local vicar would perform the ceremony. But until then, they were keeping everything a secret, and she knew that David would say nothing about their engagement. When Eleanor arrived, Katrina was kept busy, serving the meal she had made, before they did the washing up together, and it was as they sat over a cup of coffee afterwards, that she spoke up. "Are you really okay Elly?" she asked her sister. "When I phoned and talked to you, and you burst into tears, and then wouldn't talk to me afterwards, I was really worried. You kept on saying you were sorry. Sorry for what Elly? Please tell me what's wrong."

"I can't Katy. But I am sorry for everything. I lied to you when I told you about the conference. I can't tell you how boring it was. We had lectures every night, demonstrations during the day, and I learnt so much about arterial surgery, but we certainly didn't have time to go out for dinner, even if anybody had asked me. Simon was at meetings that went on until late every night, and I was in lectures, so I didn't even see him for a couple of days to talk to, just to say hello in passing. The hotel we were in, was quite a way out of the centre, too far out to do any sightseeing, and I was staying with the other SHO's who'd been invited, and we were all exhausted when the course finished." She sighed. "I knew Simon had been seeing you, I'd seen him coming out of your

block of flats one evening, and I suppose I wanted to make you jealous. So, there I was, telling you a load of lies about our trip, then he turned up in the doorway, and David was with him. You turned round, saw him, went completely white, your eyes rolled up, and the next thing, you were in a heap on the floor. The two men were so quick, I was frozen to the spot, seeing my twin sister on the floor, but they just snapped into action. David ordered me to get a trolley, and Simon put you on it, they were listening to your heart, and taking your pulse, and then they ordered me to stay where I was, and disappeared off to A&E with you. I didn't know what to do, and I'm meant to be a doctor! When they came back, they told me you were completely exhausted and you'd been admitted, before David sent me off duty. When I tried to see you that evening, the nurse wouldn't let me in, apparently David had persuaded the consultant in A&E to slap a No Visitors sign on you. Next morning, David took me into the office, and made me tell him everything I'd done to you. He was so angry, told me he'd warned me when we'd all had dinner together, when I first started working with you, and if he'd known sooner that I was trying to make you work all the hours God sent, he'd have done something about it, but he didn't say what, and that evening, I was on call, and I was so busy, I didn't have a chance to see you. I didn't desert you Katy, honest I didn't."
"I know love" Katrina took her sisters hand in hers. "Don't be daft. I didn't have time to be jealous either, because I was so busy in the department. Just having time like this, to catch up on my sleep

and the things I want to do, has been great, but I don't want to go through anything like that again." she grinned at her sister. "At least we're going to get some more staff which will be a good thing." she took a deep breath, then, "Have you heard from mum and dad? They want everybody to gather at their home for something on Thursday. They said it's important we are all there."

"Yes" Eleanor said quietly. "When I told Simon about it, he gave me the day off, told me that Steve Draper would cover me, but he didn't think they'd be busy, because he was going on annual leave that day, and said I could make up the hours23 some time. David phoned me yesterday as well, and told me to make sure I was there. I wonder what it's all about?"

"I have no idea" Katrina said, as she tried to hide the amusement she felt. She wondered what Elly would say when she found that her boss was going to be her brother-in-law! She changed the subject hurriedly, "Anybody on the horizon?" she asked. "I talked to Bella today, and she said she saw you with one of the Orthopaedic registrars again last week. She said that's the fifth or sixth time she's seen you together. Is it serious?"

"It could be" her sister admitted, then grinned properly for the first time that evening. "He's on call tonight, which is why I was able to come and have a meal with you." She looked at the clock. "And talking of which, I'd better go. You still need to have early nights to recover. You're looking a lot better than you did, but you've still got a way to go, and you need to put on some more weight, before you're completely recovered. I'm sorry for everything Katy"

She stood up, and gave her sister a big hug. “You take care won't you” she admonished her, “and I'll see you at mums on Thursday. Sleep well.” and she was gone. Left alone, Katrina pondered on her sisters visit. She had wanted to know what Elly was sorry for, but there had been no opportunity to push the subject and ask her sister, before she had gone. She hadn't noticed her engagement ring either, and she thought she would have done so. She shook her head to try and clear it. There was something else worrying her sister, something she wouldn't talk about, and Katrina hoped that her forthcoming marriage wouldn't drive a wedge between them.

Thursday morning dawned bright and clear, and Katrina knew that her wedding day was going to be good fun. Simon bought her breakfast in bed, and afterwards, she had a long bath, before getting ready for the day ahead. He drove her to her parents’ house and her mother greeted her with a smile and a kiss. “Oh Katy, your wedding day. I'm so looking forward to this, and surprising everybody” She had smiled in return, and Simon had kissed her mother saying it was normal for a man to be able to kiss his mother-in-law, and she knew that things were going to be alright. She was wearing a well-fitting suit in a light shade of green and a white blouse, and had a hat in the same colour as the suit, which she would put on later, before they arrived at the church. Simon's sisters, had arrived at her parents’ house just after they had arrived there, and although she had met them already and got on well with them, it wasn't until her siblings and their families arrived, and the whole family were together, that she felt as though their plans were coming together. James and his wife had come, and her parents were delighted to see them again, and see how well her sister-in-law's pregnancy was proceeding. David had told the entire family now, that he and Ian were a couple, and when they arrived together, the entire family welcomed Ian into their midst. It was noticeable that Eleanor didn't talk to her brother and his partner very much, but nobody said anything derogatory, which made Katrina very happy for her eldest brother. Her father had taken them all to a restaurant for a meal, and it was as they were drinking their coffee, that Eleanor asked why her parents had wanted the entire family to be together. "And why are Ian, Simon and his sisters here, if it's a family occasion?" she asked, then apologised to them. "Sorry, that sounded a bit nasty, and I didn't mean it like that, but I just wondered why?" Her father shook his head. "Eleanor, for a clever girl, you can be remarkably dumb sometimes. I think everybody else has worked it out. Today is Katrina and Simon's wedding day. We're all heading off to the church after we've eaten, and we're going to watch them get married. Didn't you notice her engagement ring?" Eleanor looked shocked, before she turned to her sister. "You never said a word" she said to her. "Had he asked you to marry him, before we went to Amsterdam?" Katrina shook her head. "No, we'd been seeing each other before then, but he didn't ask me, until after I collapsed. We didn't tell a soul, but David knew, because he saw us when we were having a meal together, just after Simon had given me my engagement ring. I'm sorry Elly, we just wanted to keep it a secret from everybody, and I was going to tell you, but you never noticed my ring when you came to have dinner with me last week, so I kept it a secret." There was a lot of laughter at that comment, and although Eleanor didn't say anything, the expression on her face, made Katrina uneasy, but she didn't say anything, as they sat together, before it was time to go, and they all headed to their cars, to go to the church. As Simon drew up outside the church, he took Katrina's hand in his. "No second thoughts?" he asked, but she shook her head. "I can't wait to become your wife" she said. "I love you so very much." He kissed her then, and watched as she donned her hat, before they went into the old building. There were flowers waiting for her at the back of the church, and he smiled as he picked them up, handed them to her, and watched as she inhaled their perfume. "I wanted you to have a proper wedding, even though it's a small one" he murmured, as their guests settled themselves into their places in the church, and then the vicar arrived, and the service began. Her father led her up the aisle to where Simon waited and she knew that they were both very happy that their families were there to see them married. When it was complete, and she was married to Simon, the registers signed and photographs taken, she felt completely happy, and judging by the expression of her families faces, they were pleased for her. She had seen David and Ian holding hands, as she and Simon walked down the aisle, and felt glad that her brother was happy with his partner. More photos were taken outside the church, her family hugged her, before they left for a short honeymoon, and as Eleanor gave her sister a big hug, Katria felt as if her sister were pleased for her. "Don't say anything about this in theatres, will you?" she begged. "We want to surprise everybody if we can."

"I promise Katy. Be happy, won't you?"

"I will" she promised. "You'll be next anyway." Eleanor watched and waved, as Simon escorted Katrina to his car, and they drove away to the hotel in Stow on the Wold, where he had taken her before he went off to Amsterdam, where they would stay for a few days.

They had been married for six days, and had returned to Simon's house, before returning to work on Monday morning, and were settling in well, when Katrina had a phone call from her mother. "Darling" she said now, "I'm really sorry to bother you, when you're still on your honeymoon, but we've got a problem. Your father has come down with a chest infection. Oh, don't worry, he's okay, but I don't want him to go out until he's really better. But the problem is that Eleanor is here as well, and she's come down with it as well. She had started it before she arrived, but the problem is, she hasn't got any clothes here, because she was only visiting for a day, when she felt so unwell, and I won't let her go back to the hospital. She's lost her voice, which is why I'm asking if you can do her a little favour. As you said that you and Simon would come and visit us tomorrow or Saturday, I wondered if you would be able to go and collect some clothes for her, from her

room in the doctors' quarters. Mainly night things, underwear and something warm for her to wear when she's up and about." Simon had been listening to the conversation, and nodded to her. "It will only take a short while" he said, "We can go now, and be back in time to go out for dinner. Tell your mother that's what we'll do. Oh, what about the keys to her room?"
"I can borrow them from the warden" she said, "as I'm her sister." Simon nodded and within a very short time, they arrived at the hospital. As he parked the car in the consultant's car park, she smiled at him. "If anybody sees us, they're going to guess what's happened, and spoil the surprise." Simon thought for a moment, then grinned at her. "They won't, if we go in separately" he said. "You go and get the keys from the warden, and I'll come to the quarters in a while, when I've been to my office to collect some papers." She agreed, and swiftly walked through the hospital to the home warden's office. Once she had explained the situation to the other woman, she was shown into Eleanor's room, and swiftly started to gather together some clothes and toiletries for her sister. She was opening the bottom drawer of the chest of drawers to get a couple of jumpers out, when Simon arrived and shut the door behind him swiftly in case anybody was watching. "Have you found everything you wanted?" he asked, and she nodded. "Just looking for something to put them in now" she replied, as she shut the drawer, and went to the wardrobe. On the top shelf was Eleanor's case, and she pulled it off`, put it on the bed and opened it. As she did so,

some envelopes and postcards fell out, and she picked one up and looked at it. She was silent for a moment, and Simon, sensing that she had seen something that disturbed her, came across to her. "What's the problem?" he said. "What have you found?"
"This" she said, "and these" and she picked up the cards and letters before showing them to him. Simon looked at them, and gasped. "These are the cards and letters I sent to you from Amsterdam" he said slowly. "What the hell is Eleanor doing with them? And how did she get hold of them? I handed them in at the hotel concierge desk, to post them to you every day. The only time I didn't was once when I was walking to the conference centre, and I 'd forgotten to hand it in, so I posted it on the way." He gasped, then "I've just realised, the one card you did get, was the one I posted myself. Do you think she took them from the concierge desk and kept them herself?" Katrina nodded. "I think she must have done. But Simon, why? Why on earth did she do it?" He shook his head, "I don't know" he said eventually. "She's your sister, has she ever done anything like this before?"
"I don't think so. I didn't get many letters when we were living at home, and after I started training, all my mail went to the nurse's home, when I was living in, or the flat after I moved out, so she wouldn't have had access to any of my mail."
"We'll probably never know why she did it," Simon said, as he sat down on the bed, and moved the case away, to make himself more comfortable. As he did so, the case slid onto the floor, and he swore to

himself, as he bent to pick it up. The internal pocket had opened, and a large brown envelope fell out. It was a thick packet, it had postage stamps on it, although they had not been franked, and obviously contained several documents, and he turned it over to look at the address. Katrina glanced at it, and gasped. “Simon” she said, “this is my application for medical school” She was white with shock, and he pushed her into the one chair in the room. “Take some deep breaths” he commanded. “I'll get you a drink,” and he took one of the cups on the tray, and filled it with water, before handing it to her. She drank it down thirstily, and then sat back in the chair. “Are you sure this is your application?” he asked and she nodded. “It's my handwriting on the envelope” she said, “and I remember I had to alter the address, because I had made a mistake, and I'd written the postcode wrong. Look” she pointed at the written address, “there's the alteration I made.” He looked closely at it, and shook his head. “Do you remember going to post it yourself” he asked, and she shook her head as she tried to remember back into the past. “No,” she said, after a while. “No, Elly said she'd post both of them. She said she'd been asked to post some letters for Dad at the same time, and I gave her the money for registering our applications. I remember that, because she said she was very hard up, at the time, as she always was, and I'd still got some money left, so she took both the letters, and when she came back afterwards, she had the receipt from the post office, so I could see how much it had cost. Simon, why on earth didn't she post it? It’s got the stamps on it, so all she had to do was hand it

over. She knew how upset I was when I didn't get an answer to the application, and she swore that she'd sent them both off at the same time. Why would she do something like this to me? I thought we were friends, we were certainly close, twins are you know." Simon was holding the envelope between his hands, as he thought about the situation, and eventually shook his head. "We are certainly going to have to ask her why she did it?" he said in the end. "But if she's got a chest infection and lost her voice, she won't be able to talk much will she? Why don't we pack everything up now, take the case home, I'll take you out to dinner tonight, and tomorrow, we'll take the case to your mum's house and see if she's got a voice, and we can ask her then. We can't do anything about it now, and I don't want you to be too upset tonight." He kissed her gently as he stood up and she got out of the chair and put her arms around his neck. "You're so sensible" she said, as she kissed him, and he held her close to him, kissing her deeply. There was a knock on the door, and they broke apart, as it opened, and the warden stood in the doorway. "Have you finished yet, Sister Howarth?" she asked, and Katrina nodded. "Just got to put the clothes in the case, and I'll be off." she replied, and smiled at the woman. "Good afternoon, Mrs. Walton" Simon said from behind the door, and the warden jumped in fright. "Oh Mr. Parker" the woman said. "I didn't see you there. Is everything alright?"
"Everything's okay" he assured her. "I came to collect some papers from my office, and somebody told me that Sister Howarth was here, so I came to

see how she was getting on. She's meant to be coming back to work soon, and I want to make sure she's fit enough to be able to work." The warden smiled at her, and watched as Katrina folded the clothes neatly into the case. Simon had picked up the envelopes scattered on the bed, and put them with the papers he had bought from his office, and now he turned to go. "Goodbye Sister Howarth" he said formally. "I'm glad to see that you're fully fit again. See you on Monday I hope." and with a nod to the warden, he walked away. Katrina shut the case, and stood upright. "Thanks for letting me come and collect everything my sister needs" she said, as she handed the keys back to the warden. "I hope she'll be back to work soon," the warden said, "and give her my best wishes won't you. She's such a nice girl and so helpful." Katrina picked up the case, thanked the warden, and accompanied by her, went to the front door and walked away.

When she reached the car park, Simon was waiting for her, and he came and took the case from her. "That was a bit of a close call" he laughed at her, as she got into the car, and ducked down so as not to be seen. "Hopefully we won't see anybody else we know". They drove away, and as they left, he breathed a sigh of relief. "We want to surprise everybody on Monday morning, don't we?" he laughed at her. "How are we going to do that?"
"I have no idea" she said, knowing he was trying to take her mind off the discovery they had made. "I could come into the theatres, and kiss you" he said with a grin, but she shook her head. "No, don't do

that" she said. "Let's not say anything to anybody, until somebody notices the wedding rings. I won't be able to wear my engagement ring into work, but nurses tend to watch other people when they are scrubbing up, and if I have to move my wedding ring to scrub under it, then somebody is going to notice. And of course, you put your hand down, as you make the incision, and the ring is going to be quite distinctive. Somebody is bound to see it, and if they don't, then we can say something at the end of the day." They laughed together, and drew up outside their house. He carried the case inside, placed it in the hall, shut the door behind them and pushed the coat from her shoulders. "Stop wondering what happened" he ordered. "Let's have a drink, then you can go and get changed into something suitable for dancing in, and I'm going to take you out to celebrate that we've been married for almost one week." and he bent and kissed her hard. She returned the kiss, and felt his need of her, as he held her close to him. "On second thoughts" he muttered against her lips, "let's forget the drink." She smiled, agreed, and led the way upstairs.

He took her to a restaurant away from the hospital, where a band played, and that evening, for a while, she managed to forget the envelopes she had found in her sister's case. Simon held her close against him, as they danced, they ate glorious food, and he kept her glass of wine topped up. "I know what you're doing" she said, as they waltzed around the floor, and he smiled at her. "And what's that?" he asked, as he drew her close to him. "You're trying to get me tiddly" she giggled, but he didn't deny it, as they danced again, and smiled at her words. "But it's fun, isn't it?" he asked her, and she nodded. They drove home, and it was as he opened the front door of the house, and escorted her inside, she saw the case he had placed in the hallway, and her mood changed, but he wouldn't allow her to think about it, and took her into the sitting room, and went into the kitchen to make her coffee. "I told you, we're not going to speculate any more tonight." he said, when he came back in and handed her the cup. "Tonight is ours, and in a minute, I'm going to take you up to bed, and make passionate love to you, and then you're going to sleep all night. Tomorrow we'll talk to your sister and ask her what happened, and we can worry about things then." The coffee was forgotten, as he bent his head, and kissed her deeply, pulled her towards him, and they ended up in each other's arms, lying on the settee, as they caressed and kissed each other, and Katrina forgot about anything else, as she gave herself up to the ecstasy her husband always made her feel.

Chapter Nine

The following morning, after they had eaten a leisurely breakfast, they got ready to go and see her parents. As Simon put the case into the boot of the car, he smiled at her. "I'm going to be with you all the time" he said quietly, "and I expect your parents will be there as well. Your mum and dad are going to want to know what happened, because I know your dad wanted you to go to medical school. He told me when you were in hospital. They couldn't understand what had happened to the application either, especially as it was so important that it was sent by registered mail. Or not" he said angrily, then in a different voice. "Katy, can you really say you've been unhappy about having trained as a nurse, instead of going to medical school?" She thought for a while, before he started the engine. "No," she said eventually. "If I'd gone to medical school, I might never have met you, because I might not have gone to the same hospital as you to work, and I would have missed my chance of happiness with you. I'd wanted to be a doctor, and I knew how much work it entailed, but I did love doing my training as a nurse, and I love doing my job, except when I have to deal with stroppy surgeons," and she grinned over at Simon, "but, yes, I was very unhappy at the start. If I'd known that Elly had held back my application, I think I'd have done something very nasty to her." She sighed, as she sat back in the seat. "I just want to know why she did it. Does she hate me so much?" Simon leant forward and took her in his arms. "She doesn't hate you, darling, I really hope she doesn't. I

was wondering if she was jealous of you."
"What's she got to be jealous of me for?" Katrina asked, but he shook his head then bent and kissed her gently. "I've got absolutely no idea. Let's go to your parents' house, and we can get her to explain." She nodded, and he started the engine, and they drove off.

When they drew up outside her parent' house, he stopped the engine, took her hand in his, and leant across to kiss her. "Don't worry" he said quietly, "Go and talk to your mum, and I'll have a chat to your father, and see how he suggests we do this. Try not to be too angry with Elly at the moment, if she's with your mother, and I'll soon be with you." She smiled at him, and they got out of the car, retrieved the case from the boot, and went up the path to the front door. Katrina was totally unprepared to find David present, with her mother in the kitchen. "What are you doing here?" she asked, as she grinned at him. "Or did you just want to come and see how we are?" He shook his head, "I didn't know you were coming today. I wanted to have a chat with mum about something, and she told me you were coming, so I thought I'd stay and see how you are enjoying married life?" He grinned at her widely, so that she forgot about the upcoming questions, and smiled back. "Very nice thank you" she said demurely. "I'm going back to work on Monday, so we're trying to make sure that nobody knows about us, until we announce it. We're not going to say anything, unless somebody notices our wedding rings, and if nobody does, then we'll tell everybody before we go home."

Her mother smiled at her, and went to put the kettle on, and she took the opportunity to ask her brother how his relationship was going. "That's what I wanted to talk to Mum about?" he said. "Ian and I have decided to form a civil partnership, or even get married, we've found a house we like, so we're going to buy it and move in together, and I wondered what they felt about it."

"Oh Dave, that's brilliant news" she cried, as she embraced her brother. "I was really hoping that you and he would be happy together, and I'm so pleased for you both." He held her close to him and gave her a hug. "Thanks Katy" he whispered. "You've got no worries about us, have you?"

"Of course I haven't. It's obvious you are so right for each other" she said. "Just be happy together won't you, and that will make me very happy. You will let me know when you've decided on a date won't you? I really want to be there for you."

"Of course I'll let you know. I was hoping you might be involved as a ring bearer, if we decide to marry. I want everybody to be there." he stopped, then went on, "I don't know whether or not Elly will want to be with us. She wasn't too polite when I told her what Ian and I were planning. She called me some rather nasty names as well. I didn't realise how intolerant she was about things like that."

"Do you want me to talk to her?" Katy said, then having remembered what she and Simon were going to talk to her sister about later on, she hesitated. "Actually, I don't know whether or not she'd listen to me." she said. "Simon and I need to talk to her today, providing she's got her voice back, and as

you're here, perhaps you'd listen in, and act as an arbitrator?"
David looked quizzically at her. "What's the problem?" he asked, but she shook her head. "You'll hear later on." she said, "Where is she?"
"Upstairs in her room."
"And has she got her voice back?" she asked and David nodded at her question. "Yes, but she might have lost it again after this morning, when she yelled at me, and told me I was disgusting, a pervert and a disgrace to the family."
"She didn't?" Katrina said, astounded at her sisters' attitude, then shook her head. "I don't know what's got into her lately" she said quietly. "I'd stay around if I were you, and listen out for the fireworks." Her mother had been busy, but now she was carrying a tray with teacups on it, and grinned at her daughter. "Has David told you his good news?" she asked and Katrina nodded. "Yes, and I'm delighted for him" she said, then, "shall I call Dad and Simon in to have a drink?" Her mother nodded, and Katrina went to her father's study. Her father looked closely at her as she opened the door. "Tea is served in the kitchen" she said, but when she would have left, he closed the door behind her. "Simon has just showed me what you found in Elly's room. Why on earth would she do something like that?"
"I have no idea" Katrina said quietly. "But I really want to know. Let's go and have a cup of tea, and then we can ask her." Her father put his arm around her shoulder and gave her a hug. "You're being very calm about it" he said, "and I'm proud of you. Try to keep your temper as long as you can, and remember,

she is still your twin, and she must have had a good reason, or what she thought was a good reason."
"I'll try Dad, I promise. Simon can hold me back, if I decide to smack her, can't you?" and she looked up at him, and they exchanged a smile. They went back into the hall, and her mother looked up as they came into the kitchen. "Give Elly a shout, please Katy" she said, and Katrina went back into the hallway, and called up the stairs to her sister. "Elly, teas poured out. Come down and see me." She could hear noises upstairs, as the bedroom door opened, and her sister came to the top of the stairs. "Come down, and have a cup of tea with us" Katrina said, and her sister nodded, and started to walk down the stairs towards her. Katrina hugged her sister and then led her towards the kitchen. There was a slight pause in the conversation, as the two girls walked into the room, and Simon smiled at them both. "No wonder my patients are being neglected, if you decide to take a day off for no apparent reason." he laughed at her, but Eleanor didn't smile back. "I had no voice at all yesterday" she said, huskily, "I also had a temperature, and I didn't think you'd appreciate it if I gave all your patients' chest infections, which would have delayed their surgery even more than it has done by you being on annual leave."
"I'm joking Elly," he said, and she nodded, then went to stand by the sink, as far away from David and Simon, as she could get. It was very noticeable that she didn't join in any of the conversations that were going on, and looking at her, Katrina could see that her sister was very tense and didn't appear to be very happy. She was very reserved as well, and her

demeanour was so different to what it normally was, that she was unwilling to ask her the questions she knew she was going to have to. Her father smiled at his family, and said, "Come and sit down, we might as well be comfortable, while we have tea and a chat" and then led the way to the sitting room. Simon was last, unwilling to let Eleanor leave the group and go back upstairs to her room, so he waited until her mother had handed round the tea cups and when they were all settled into comfortable chairs, he stood in front of the door. "I've got a question to ask you Elly" he said quietly, and took from his pocket, the bundle of letters and cards which he had sent to Katy, but which had been intercepted by Eleanor. "Just wondered why you had these?" he asked, "especially when they were meant to have been posted from the hotel in Amsterdam." Eleanor went white, and didn't say anything, until her father tapped her on the knee. "Why Elly?" he asked. "Why did you keep them back?"
Eleanor looked up swiftly, then cast her eyes down to the floor, before she spoke, her voice husky and low, a hangover from her chest infection. "I wanted to make Katy jealous" she said "I thought it would be a laugh if I stopped them being sent, so I told the concierge that she was my sister and I was having a joke with her. He fancied me, and thought it would be a laugh as well, and gave me the cards and letters without me having to ask him for them."
"So why did you want to make her jealous?" Simon asked, and for the first time, Katrina saw something in her sisters' eyes that made her feel cold inside. "I

saw you coming out of her block of flats one evening. I guessed you'd been seeing her, and I wanted to make it appear that you'd fallen for me, instead of for her. You wouldn't respond to me at all, when I tried to get you interested, and I suppose I was jealous. She gets everything, and I get nothing." she burst out, and Katy gasped. "Don't talk such rot" she said. "You've got everything you ever wanted, and you certainly haven't lacked for male company. Every time I tried to arrange for us to spend an evening together when you first came to the hospital, you were off out with somebody. I've been informed that you've been taken out very frequently while you've been at Queens, and what about your current beau, the orthopaedic registrar, the one you admitted could be serious? And come to that, what about John? You got him, didn't you?" Eleanor just glared at her sister, but didn't say anything, and Simon interrupted them both. "Okay, so you just did it as a laugh. A good job that Katy didn't worry about it. But, on a more serious note, what explanation have you got for this then?" and he
3 produced the envelope that contained her application for medical school. David frowned as he looked at it, and asked "What's in it?" Simon handed it to David who took out the contents. Katrina's brother looked through them, and his eyes hardened as he realised what it was. "Where the hell did you find it?" he asked as he handed the documents to their mother, who looked at them, and gasped as she saw what they were. "They'd been hidden in the inside pocket of Eleanor's case" Simon said coldly. "When Katy and I went to collect some clothes for

Eleanor, from her room in the doctors' house, she put the case on the bed, and it fell off, and this envelope came to light. So, what have you got to say for yourself Eleanor? You told Katy, you'd posted the letter, hell, it's even got stamps on it, so you must have taken it back after you'd paid the postage, and you've kept it hidden for the last ten or eleven years. Katy told me you'd sympathised with her about the fact that it had gone missing, yet you knew where it was all the time. You made Katy lose her place at medical school, and you watched while she had to go and train as a nurse, while you swanned off to medical school, qualified and then rubbed it in big time, when you applied for the scholarship to come and work with me, while you knew that Katy was the theatre sister in the unit. You've tried to make her jealous, tried to break us up, by hiding all the letters I wrote to her while I was in Amsterdam, and I know damn well, because I've been present on some of the occasions, that you were one of the people who would persuade her to stay after her time, in order to scrub for the cases that you wouldn't cancel, even when you had been specifically told that they couldn't be done. You knew she wasn't able to produce enough staff to cover the lists, but you tried to make sure that she always had to stay late. No wonder she became ill! And were you trying to make the situation worse when you first arrived, when you hid swabs during the case, or when you told her I wanted to re-order the list, or produce an operating list that had seven large cases on it? Cases that had already been done! What else have you done to her? What do you have to say for yourself Eleanor?" His voice was cold, and Katrina hoped he'd never talk to her like that. Her mother was in tears as she gazed at her youngest daughter, David was staring at her in shock, and her father had his eyes closed as he tried to assimilate what had happened. Eleanor was staring at Simon, her mouth opening and closing, but no sound was emerging. She was chalk white, her eyes very dark in her face, and although Katy felt sorry for her, she wanted to know what had caused her sister to behave as she had done. "Come on Elly" David said quietly, "I think we all want to know what you were thinking about? Why on earth did you do it?" Eleanor sat up straight and glared at Katy and Simon. "Because she's always appeared better than me, and I wanted her to be shown up in a bad light. Everybody liked her more than they did me, she was always the most popular one at school, she had the steady boyfriends, and I didn't. My boyfriends didn't seem to last beyond one or two dates. That's why I took John from her. He became infatuated with me, and asked me to marry him instead. He didn't like it when I told him I didn't want to marry him after all! It just proved that I could take him away from her. And now she's got married before me as well! Mum and Dad like her more than they do me. I wanted to make her realise that she wasn't infallible, if I kept back her application, then she'd realise that I could do something that she couldn't do. I was going to send it off the following year, but she was nursing by then and doing well, so I decided to keep it" she spat the answer at him, and Katy gasped. Her mother and father were looking stunned. "Don't be so silly" her father said, "we don't have favourites, you are as precious to us, as Katy is, as all our children are special."

"Then why did you always introduce her to your friends before me, - it was always Katy and Elly, not Elly and Katy, you'd tell them how well she did at school, when I'd done just as well, but no, you and mum didn't realise it, you always put me second. She was always the one who did better than me. I'm glad I hid the envelope, and it's just bad luck that it's come to light now. But she did alright, didn't she? You probably don't realise you're doing it, but even now, its Katrina, the Theatre Sister, not Eleanor, the doctor. Why don't you realise that for once, I've done better than her? I've qualified and I'm working as a doctor, but no, it's always Katy, the Gold medallist, Katy the nurse. And then in front of Simon's sisters and his" and she nodded at David, and spat out the word, "boyfriend, you called me dumb." She turned her head away, and stared at the floor, "and, you won't hear a word said against David and his boyfriend, and it's disgusting, it's not natural, none of it is."

"Elly!" her mother said, but her sister wouldn't listen to anything, and she sprang up to leave the room, but Simon was there in front of her, stopping her.

"Don't be so stupid" her father said again as he walked across the room and took her in his arms. "Elly, we've never favoured Katy above you. We are proud of you both, and if you'd both qualified as doctors, we'd have been overjoyed. We're very proud that you managed to go through the hard work and the training and become a doctor, and we've told all our friends about how proud we are of you, winning this scholarship, to work with Simon. And believe me, we don't think that David's relationship with Ian is unnatural. We're very happy for him, and you should be happy too." Eleanor was sobbing hard, not listening to her father, but he was holding her close to him, as he told her again and again, that they were very proud of her, that they hadn't realised that she felt so deeply about it, and eventually her sobs died, and her mother handed her some tissues to wipe her face. Katy was on her feet, her eyes full of tears, and Simon came to stand with her, and hold her close. "Leave them to it, I think" he muttered, and opened the door, and they went into her father's study, accompanied by David, who looked as shocked as they all felt. "Why?" Katy said now, "Why did she feel like that? Mum and Dad always treated us both equally. I never had more than she did, and I know that they were so proud of her when she qualified. We even had a big party for her, didn't we Dave? I only got taken out for a celebratory meal, when I passed my exams." Her brother nodded, "Yes, they arranged it and got all the relatives to come and celebrate with us. The champagne flowed quite lavishly that evening, as I recall."

"Yes, we all had bad headaches the following day, didn't we?" Katy smiled in remembrance, then her face fell. "She's my twin sister, and I love her, but to hear that, was a complete shock." Simon gave her a hug, "I can't imagine how that felt, hearing that" he said quietly. "I didn't envisage anything like that, when I asked your father what we should do about it."

"So, what are we going to do?" David asked, but Simon shook his head, "I've got no idea" he said quietly. "Perhaps we all ought to leave her with your parents, so they can talk to her, and try and make her feel better than she does at the moment. And Dave, believe me, both Katy and I are proud to call you and Ian, friends, and we're delighted that you're going to make it official. And neither of us share Elly's views about you, and we heard what your parents think about you both."
"Thanks Simon" David said, and looked relieved. He agreed on their course of action, and Simon smiled at them both. "I'll go and whisper to anybody who's free, that we'll phone them later on, and find out what's happening." and he went to the door, but Katrina's mother was there before he could open it. "Katy, I'm so sorry" she said, "I had absolutely no idea that she felt like that, and to hide your application, well, I can't believe it. But you do know that your father and I are very proud of you, don't you?"
"Don't worry mum" Katrina said, as she nodded. "Simon, Dave and I will go now. You go and look after Elly. Phone us later on, and let us know what's happened." Her mother kissed them all, and they left the house. Katrina stood looking up at the front of the house. "I was always happy here" she said, "but after today, I don't think I want to come back too often. Scenes like that, make you feel that everything that happened before was a complete act." Simon gave her a kiss on the cheek. "Give it time," he said. "You won't always feel like that." David agreed, but Katrina wanted nothing more than

to get back to Simon's house, where she now felt completely at home. "I'll take Katy back home" Simon told David, and he nodded his agreement, and gave his sister a hug, then watched as Simon opened the door for her, and got in beside her, and drove off. He shook his head, as he got into his own car, and drove back to Ian's house, longing to be able to talk to his partner about the situation and discuss what they should do about it.

When they arrived back at Simon's house, Katy got out of the car, and opened the door of the house, before going into the kitchen, to put the kettle on. Simon came in behind her, and watched for a second, before he came up behind her, and put his arms around her, bending his head, to kiss the back of her neck. She was crying bitterly, and he took the kettle from her unresisting hands, put it down, turned her around and held her close as she sobbed on his shoulder. "I thought she was my friend, and now it turns out, she's hated me all this time" she said eventually, but Simon shook his head. "She doesn't hate you" he said quietly, before he kissed her gently. "She's obviously ill, and it appears that she's jealous of you. There's something in her head, that has made her feel as though you're the top person, when you and everybody else can see that you've both been treated equally. I think she will need some psychiatric counselling, but I'm not going to suggest it to anybody. I'm going to leave it to your parents to make up their minds as to how they treat her." He kissed her again, and although she responded, he could feel that she wasn't fully in control of her emotions. "Try not to think about it" he suggested, but she couldn't put Eleanor's words out her mind. He kissed her again, and again, and slowly he could feel her responding further to his actions, and he knew she was going to be able to forget what had happened for a while, in his arms, while he made love to her, and slowly he led her up the stairs to their bedroom.

Afterwards, he left Katy, worn out with differing emotions, asleep on the bed, and went downstairs to sit and think about things. He didn't know what to do about Eleanor – she was meant to be working for him, but after today's revelations, he didn't think she'd be able to work properly for a long while, and wondered whether or not to make sure she was transferred to Ewan Dexter's team, or indeed away from the hospital. It would probably be better, he thought, and smiled to himself, as he wondered if his relationship with Katy would make Eleanor's reactions worse or better. He was jolted out of his thoughts by the phone, and he swiftly answered it, not wanting Katy to be woken. Her father was on the other end of the phone, and was anxious to tell him what had happened. "After you left, she had a full-blown attack of hysterics," he said, "a very bad one. She just keeps sobbing that she's sorry for what she's done to Katy, but after the way she acted, I don't know whether to believe that statement." Simon listened to the other man for a while. "What have you done for her since we left?" he asked, and was reassured. "I've contacted a colleague of mine, a psychiatrist, and he straight away, came and saw her. He's given her a very strong sedative, and she should sleep now until the morning. He's going to take her under his wing, and look after her. He's going to get her admitted to a hospital, under his care. But Simon, I think you're going to have to do without an SHO for quite a while. She won't be fit enough to work for a few weeks, and it's probably going to take a lot longer than that to get her to accept that there's no basis of truth in her thoughts. I'm going to suggest that she leaves Queens, and goes back to St. Anselm's, or better still, to another hospital, somewhere there are no memories for her, nothing for her to compare with Katy. I don't know why she behaved as she did – her mother and I treated them just the same. I wonder if it was because she's the youngest, by all of ten minutes" he added "that made her feel like that."

"Don't worry John" Simon said quietly. "I've already decided that she won't be able to come back onto my team at Queens, and I was going to suggest that she goes back to St. Anselm's. I wonder if your colleague could contact me, and we can decide what to tell the hospital authorities? We don't want anybody else to know the truth about it, for her sake." John Howarth agreed, then, "How's Katy? It must have upset her." Simon smiled, although the other man couldn't see him. "It did, but she's had a good cry, and she's upstairs asleep at the moment. I'll try to make her understand that she need feel no blame for the situation, when she wakes up." The two men chatted on for a minute, before saying their goodbyes, and Simon replaced the receiver. "I don't feel any blame" Katy said from the doorway. She

was in her dressing gown, her hair rumpled, where Simon's hands had run through it, and her eyes were red, where she had been crying, but she looked a lot better than she had done, and he came to where she stood, and held her close to him. "I woke up shortly after you came downstairs, and I've been lying and thinking about what happened. She's not well, is she? Will Dad try and get her some help, do you think?"
"He's doing just that" he said, and kissed her gently. "Your parents are worried about you, but I hope I reassured them, that I'll be able to look after you and they won't need to worry about you too much."
"You're too good to me" she said, as she reached up to kiss his cheek. "I love you so much, and I'm so grateful that you love me. Do you reckon that our marriage has pushed Elly over the edge, as it were?"
Simon shook his head. "No, I don't. Her jealousy goes back to when you were very young, before you started school, before you even thought about boys, and has been there for a long, long time. I think the fact that you collapsed in front of her, when Dave and I were there, shocked her, and made her realise what she'd done, which is why she kept on apologising to you when you phoned her." Katy nodded, "She said the evening she came to the flat for dinner, she'd done some stupid things, but things had gone too fast for her, and she hadn't been able to undo them. I didn't understand then, but I do now. Poor Elly" she added. "What's going to happen now? Is she going to be on sick leave for a while?"
Simon nodded. "Your father and I think it might be a good idea if she goes to another hospital, when she's

better, one where you've never worked, so there's nothing to remind her of you, when she's considered well enough to go back to work, if she wants to continue working as a doctor." He sighed as he held her close. "But I don't think she'll be at Dave's partnership ceremony. I can't believe that she's as intolerant as she let on this morning. She's obviously kept that bottled up for a long time. But that might be part of her problem. Poor Elly" he said and she smiled at him. "Thank you" she said simply, and he looked at her. "What for?" he asked, but she just said, "everything" and wouldn't say any more.

On Monday morning, Simon woke Katy up with a kiss, and watched as she got ready for work. "It's going to be difficult today" he said, and she turned to face him. "Why?" she asked, and he held her close. "Because I'm going to want to hold you close to me every time I see you, and kiss and caress you, and instead I've got to call you Sister Howarth, and behave as if you mean nothing to me." She grinned at him. "Until somebody notices the wedding rings" she said, and he kissed her deeply again. "Don't start anything" she warned him. "I've got to be in theatres by 7.30, and I won't be, if you do that."
"Spoilsport" he said, before kissing her on the cheek again, and watching as she got ready for the day ahead. She wondered if anything would be said about her sister's absence, for Eleanor had been admitted to a hospital, and was receiving treatment, and she knew that it was the best place for her, until her twin could accept the situation. They had gone downstairs to have breakfast, before they left for the

hospital, a meal taken quickly with not a lot of conversation. At last, she was ready, and they left the house together. They had discussed their arrival at the hospital the day before, and he had agreed to take her to the flat so she could walk in, and not arrive with him. As he drew up outside the block of flats, he bent and kissed her hard. "I love you" he murmured, as she opened the door to get out. "I'll see you in theatre later on." and he watched as she walked swiftly towards the hospital.

When she arrived in the theatre unit, she met the night nurse, who greeted her with a smile. "It's lovely to see you back Katrina" she said, and she took the report from her then the two girls talked for a while, as Deirdre wanted to know how she was. Katrina told her, and the two girls parted when the rest of the day staff came on duty. "Oh Katrina" cried Bella, when she walked into the office and found her friend and senior present, before giving her a hug. "It's so good to have you back and see that you're okay. Did you do anything while you were off sick?"
Katrina shook her head. "Nothing worth mentioning" she said, crossing her fingers as she lied to her friend, "Just spent a lot of time sleeping, eating and recovering. I feel so much better than I did." Bella smiled at her, "I can understand a bit more, how things must have got on top of you. What with the reduced lists and the extra staff, I was able to do some, but I didn't realise just how much paperwork there is in a department like this."
"Complicated, isn't it?" Katrina said with a smile, and

the two girls discussed the work list. "Do you need me to scrub?" she asked, but Bella shook her head. "Not this morning" she said, "but you could share Mr. Parker's list this afternoon if you wanted to."

"Oh, how nice to be able to have a chance to do the office paperwork" Katrina said, with a grimace, and the two girls laughed together, and Katrina went to the office to get on with the work that awaited her. She was sorting out some of the papers she needed to have a good look at when a voice spoke from the doorway. "Good morning, Sister. Are you feeling better now?" was the greeting that came from Simon who was standing in the doorway, and she looked at him and smiled. "Good morning, Mr. Parker. Yes, thank you, I'm fine now." she answered, and blew him a kiss, unseen by Joe who was standing behind him. "Any problems?" he asked, but she shook her head. "None at all, thank you for asking" she said,

"Well, it's nice to have you back" he said, and he left her to go and get changed. She had gone into the theatre where he was working to give a message to the anaesthetist, when the patient was ready for surgery, and as he picked up the scalpel, and asked if it were okay to start, she decided she would wait for a while. He placed his left hand flat on the patients' body, and prepared to make the incision, when the scrub nurse, Anne, saw his wedding ring and said loudly, "You've got married!" then ducked her head in embarrassment. Simon grinned at her, and nodded. "Guilty as charged" he said. "I got married on Thursday, when I started my holiday, and last week was our honeymoon." Joe gasped at his

statement.
"You didn't tell anybody you were going to get married" he said. "We'd all have liked to be present to see you caught." There was a chorus of agreements and congratulations from everybody around him, as he started to operate, and Katy knew that her staff were speculating about who he had married, but nobody said anything else, until the end of the operation, and Katrina had come back into the theatre, to talk to one of the other nurses, when Joe said softly, "Who are you married to?" and Simon shot him a quizzical glance.
"Who do you think I should be married to?" he asked, and looked directly at Katrina. Joe followed his gaze, and saw Katrina smile at Simon, saw too, her wedding ring, and everything clicked into place. Joe said loudly. "So why weren't we invited Katrina?" and everybody turned to look at her. She was smiling as she answered him. "We wanted to keep it a secret" she said. "The only people present were our families." She couldn't say anything else, for her staff were congratulating her, for she was a very popular person, and they realised that she and Simon were perfectly matched. The rest of the day passed quickly, with no problems, and when she was preparing to go home that evening, and Simon came into the office, she knew she had enjoyed her first day as Sister Parker, instead of as Sister Howarth, and with Simon's love surrounding her, she would continue to enjoy her days as his wife.

THE END

Printed in Great Britain
by Amazon

48745911R00108